party of five™

Sarah: don't say you love me

ROSALIND NOONAN

BASED ON THE TELEVISION SERIES CREATED BY CHRISTOPHER KEYSER & AMY LIPPMAN

AN ARCHWAY PAPERBACK
Published by POCKET BOOKS
New York London Toronto Sydney Tokyo Singapore

AN ARCHWAY PAPERBACK *Original*

An Archway Paperback published by
POCKET BOOKS, a division of Simon & Schuster Inc.
1230 Avenue of the Americas, New York, NY 10020

A PARACHUTE BOOK

ISBN: 0-671-02452-3

First Archway paperback printing October 1998

10 9 8 7 6 5 4 3 2 1

Printed in the U.S.A.

Sarah: don't say you love me

Chapter 1

Sarah?" Bailey called from outside my room.

"I'm in here," I replied. I didn't take my eyes off the screen of my laptop. My fingers flew over the keyboard as I pieced together an essay for my criminal justice course at Berkeley. I'm a freshman there.

I heard my door swing open. "Sarah? Oh, not the computer again," Bailey moaned.

"Mmmm," I mumbled.

"Why can't we have a conversation without you being glued to that gray box?" he complained. The irritation in his voice prompted me to look up. Bailey leaned against the doorjamb, his solid frame filling the space.

Bailey Salinger, my best friend in the whole world, is this teddy bear of a guy with short brown hair, a strong, square jaw, and amazing blue eyes. The kind that can make your heart melt.

1

But as far as romance stuff, we've been there, done that. Through it all we managed to stay close. In fact, right now we're sharing an apartment.

"I'm going to go pick up some Chinese food, and I thought you might want some," Bailey offered, "but I see you're lost in computer la-la land."

"It's something for school," I said. "Sort of an examination of our system of incarceration as punishment. Does the daily life of a criminal behind bars address the crime?"

"Oh." Bailey nodded. "Whatever."

Can you tell that he's not exactly enthralled by academia?

"Do you want egg rolls?" he asked, glancing at the menu in his hand. "Sesame noodles? Chow fun is always fun."

I started to reach for the menu, then shook my head. "There's a peanut butter sandwich in the kitchen with my name on it."

It's not like there's any contest between a peanut butter sandwich and noodles with spicy peanut sauce. But I had to stick to my budget, or I wouldn't be able to come up with next semester's tuition.

Takeout Chinese would cost me only about five bucks. But a peanut butter sandwich was less than a dollar. It doesn't sound like a huge difference, but if you save four dollars a day for a month, that's a hundred and twenty dollars. And that's enough to buy a couple of textbooks. More than a couple if you get them used.

I've practically worn out the keys on my calculator figuring all this stuff out. And I'm still not sure I'm going to make it. I'm still not sure I'm going to be able to come up with the registration fees for next semester, and if I don't—

"You're stressed," Bailey observed, interrupting my thoughts. "It's the building, isn't it? You've had to be this—this super super all week. Delivering notices, fixing everything. *I'm* going to fix that leak in the basement tonight though. I promise."

"No. It's not the building stuff." My job as super, otherwise known as building manager, with Bailey wasn't fun. But I was *not* going to complain about anything that gave me a discount on the rent.

"You're overextended. Your credit cards are maxed out," he guessed.

"Umm, no . . ." My hair slipped over my shoulders as I shook my head. I didn't think my credit cards were maxed out—yet. I didn't like to look at the statements too closely. They were totally depressing.

"You're trying to pretend everything is great, but inside you're screaming: Help me! I'm dying for an egg roll!" Bailey teased.

"Okay! All right, yes!" I laughed. "I'm having fast-food withdrawal," I admitted.

"But you're completely broke." Bailey smiled, revealing those totally cute dimples of his.

"Completely," I agreed.

Bailey has a way of figuring out exactly what's upsetting me. It's actually kind of scary.

"I think we should talk about everything that's bothering you. Really. But our brains will work better with fuel. My treat. The best plans are made over fried rice." Bailey shoved his wallet into his pocket. "Um, Sarah, if you need a loan . . ."

"Just get out of here." I threw one of my stuffed

animals at him. "And don't come back without steamed vegetable dumplings!"

The teddy bear missed by a few feet. Bailey slammed the door behind him.

It was totally, typically, sweet of Bailey to try to lend me money—even though he didn't really have much to spare. Bailey knew that money became a major concern for me the day I moved out of my parents' house.

I knew Bailey thought it was all his fault I wasn't living at home anymore. See, for a while, Bailey was drinking a lot. One night he smashed up his Jeep—and I'm the one who landed in the hospital. My parents brought a lawsuit against him. They couldn't understand that Bailey changed. He wasn't even drinking anymore when the case went to court.

That's when I packed everything I owned and left my parents' house.

I wish I could make Bailey understand that the trouble with my parents didn't start with how they treated him. The friction really began back in high school when I discovered that Dylan and Marie Reeves adopted me when I was four days old. Imagine how I felt when I realized they'd been hiding the truth from me for sixteen years. It was like they were never going to tell me.

I knew if I went to my parents and told them I was wrong about Bailey, and that I was sorry about everything, they would pay my tuition. But I didn't want that. I wasn't going to let them use their money to control me. I wasn't going to be their little Sarah doll.

I would find a way to deal with my money problems myself. I just didn't know how. I glanced down at the computer and sighed. There was no way I could work on the essay right now. My brain was too full.

I saved the file and closed the computer. I ran my fingers over the smooth top. A pang of guilt washed over me when I thought about how much this toy cost. Some kids get really excited about their first car. Some people obsess over their first apartment or their dorm room, making sure that they have matching towels and accent pillows and framed posters with a theme.

Not me. My first adult toy was my computer. The software was cutting-edge. It was fast, simple, compact—perfect for my papers and research at Berkeley.

But it wasn't going to do me much good if I couldn't come up with some money for school.

"Time to stop feeling sorry for yourself," I said aloud. I slipped off the bed.

I needed to do something positive. I needed to take action. I needed to—straighten my quilt. And—stack my mail more neatly on my dresser. I was about to give the door of my overstuffed closet a shove, when it hit me.

My clothes! The closet was brimming over with beautiful velvet dresses and knit sweaters and leather jackets that my mother bought me. Half of them still had tags dangling from their sleeves. I mean, the clothes were gorgeous. I *loved* them.

But did I really *need* them all?

My fingers glided over the buttery finish of an eggplant-colored leather jacket. Totally funky. Designer name. Your basic fashion dream. I adored it. Anyone would love to have it . . .

Including this cool thrift shop on Durant Street, I

thought. They had a reputation for paying top dollar for used clothes. And they would consider this jacket a major score.

I bet I could even take some of the brand-new clothes back to the original stores and get the full price back.

The full price—hmmm.

That settled it. You've never seen anyone fold and stack so fast. I filled three shopping bags with my fashion excess. But I knew I could do better. I glanced up at my top shelf. Of course! The boots and hats!

I leapt up to grab some stuff, when a small stationery box tumbled down. The lid fell off as it hit the floor—and out spilled a dozen letters in pale peach envelopes.

No, not love letters.

They were letters to my birth mother.

She's an actress, and her name is Robin Merrill. Sounds like a perfect celebrity name, right? For all I know, she could be a rising star on Broadway or in London. I tracked her down when I was a junior in high school. We saw each other a few times, and I thought we were really starting to connect.

Then . . . she was gone. Off touring with some road production of a play. She had promised to stay in touch. She had even given me this box of pale peach stationery, along with her cat. I mean, you would think that a person would visit or call to check on their cat.

But the day Robin took off in her car was the last I'd heard of her. She never wrote me or anything, and after a while my letters started coming back marked "Return to Sender. No Forwarding Address." I saved them all. I'm not sure why.

Now, as I picked up the faded envelopes, I felt foolish. My real mother had rejected me twice—first when she gave me up for adoption, and again when she just kind of disappeared from my life. I couldn't believe I'd been stupid enough to keep reaching out to her.

Like she cared about me. Like she cared about Amanda, the cat that had been a pretty decent pet—until it streaked off down the street one night and never came back.

Just like Robin.

Holding one of the envelopes up to the light, I frowned. Maybe writing the letters had been sort of therapeutic at the time. But right now the best therapy would be a clean break.

There was only one thing to do, so I did it. I ripped up the letters—shredded them into small pieces—and tossed them in the trash.

And you know what? I felt good about it. Sort of festive and free . . . really free.

Like I said, sometimes the best thing is a clean break.

Chapter 2

Candles flickered on the table, casting warm light over our faces. Bailey and his sister Julia were relaxed, laughing about something their four-year-old brother Owen had done that day.

The little French café oozed class and charm. Vases of yellow roses were placed here and there, and the tables were set far enough apart to give everyone a lot of privacy. If only I could relax and enjoy myself.

But I was so nervous, constantly wiping my palms on my thighs, even though the restaurant was cool and comfortable. And David Wyman, my new boyfriend, was restrained, quiet, and impossible to read. In other words, his typical self.

David is *always* hard to read. When I look into his smoky eyes I almost never have any idea what he's thinking or feeling. He's one of those serious guys who are sort of impenetrable. Like he's too strong to let anyone else in. Which is the exact thing that makes him so irresistible.

For about the millionth time I wondered what Julia and Bailey thought of David. I mean, I found David intriguing. I was always curious about what was going on in his head. But Julia and Bailey could think he was cold or maybe just plain boring.

It's so hard to bring a guy you like into an established circle of friends. David and I met in September when we'd been assigned a group project at school. We'd gone out a few times, but tonight was the first time it hadn't been just the two of us.

I wanted Bailey and Julia to like him, but I could tell he wasn't an instant hit. Partly because he barely said a word beyond "Pass the bread sticks."

"So anyway," Bailey went on, "Owen is really into Superman. And when I asked him if he wanted to go to the supermarket with me, he nodded and said, 'Yeah. I want to go to the Superman Market.'" Bailey laughed. "He cracks me up."

David didn't even smile. I don't think he's one of those guys that loves kids, like Bailey. Or maybe he was just as nervous as I was.

"So, David," Julia jumped in, "what's your take on Berkeley?"

"Pretty good so far," David answered. He glanced over at me as if I were the reason his semester was good. I felt myself blush a little. "I guess we'll know more when we get our first semester grades," he told Julia.

"Grades! Let's not get ahead of things!" I joked.

"Yeah." Bailey pretended to shudder. "Grades!"

Everyone stared at each other. Oh, great. The conversation had hit a dead end. Again.

I glanced out the window, hoping for *something* else to talk about. Sunlight was fading, and people moved quickly, their jackets buttoned against the cold.

No inspiration there. I pushed my dinner plate away. At least we'd made it through the entree. I would personally haul back my boot under the table and kick the person who dragged out this ordeal by ordering dessert.

"The chicken was good," Julia noted. She smoothed her napkin on her lap.

Thanks for trying, Julia, I thought. There had been only a few seconds of silence, but a few seconds can feel like a very long time.

"Yeah, maybe we should tell the chef at Salingers to try a raspberry sauce," Bailey added.

David *still* didn't say anything.

"Yeah. Did I mention that David has a cool car?" I blurted out. It wasn't like we'd been talking about anything even slightly related to cars, but I wanted to give David an opening to talk about something I knew he liked. "It's metallic blue. A classic car. What's it called again?"

"GTO, '76. Four on the column. Mint," David stated.

"Oh, yeah?" Bailey nodded. "Convertible?"

David nodded.

Well, I thought, that got us through another two seconds.

"It's out in the parking lot," David added.

"Really?" Bailey's eyes lit up. "Mind if I check it out?"

"No problem." David stood up. "We'll be right back." He touched my shoulder for a second, then turned and left the table.

"Go on and order dessert if you want," Bailey said. He turned away before I could glare at him.

Julia sat back against the banquette. "It's amazing. Guys never give up their toys. They just switch to more expensive models."

"Really." I drew little circles on my water glass with my finger. Time for the verdict. "So . . . what do you think?" I asked. "I mean, he's smart. Really smart. And he's got this great sense of humor. Though sometimes I guess you do have to work for a laugh."

"Hmmm," Julia began, her dark eyes thoughtful.

"I know he was really quiet tonight," I rushed on. "He's not always that way. If you heard him talk in class . . . okay, he's on the quiet side, but—"

"Sarah, do you hear yourself?" Julia interrupted. "You asked me what I thought, then you didn't give me one second to tell you. You're rambling on like a nervous talk show host."

"Oh." I took a gulp of water, then let out a breath. "I *am* nervous."

"Why? It's just Bay and me," Julia said. "We're your friends. Practically family."

"Exactly." I nodded. "In a way, you're the only family I have right now. It's not like I'm ever going to bring David home to meet my parents or anything. That's why I care—I really care what you think about him. So . . . don't hold back. Tell me what you think. Because I'm not completely sure about him. I mean, I'm ninety-nine percent sure. But sometimes, I wonder. Do you know what I mean?"

Julia laughed. "This is not the Sarah Reeves I know. What happened to the eternal optimist? The sunshine girl? The person who always sees the very best in everyone and every situation?"

"You know, that's a good question." I frowned. Was I turning into this totally negative person? There were so many things stressing me out. Maybe they were getting to me more than I realized.

Sometimes my whole life felt like a total mess. If I didn't find a way to bring in some more money, I might have to drop out of school. I was totally estranged from my adoptive parents. I couldn't even call them and just . . . talk. And my birth mom—forget about it. That situation was too sad and depressing. I didn't even have a correct address for Robin.

But I couldn't let all the garbage in my life stop me from appreciating the good stuff. Like David. I really did like him. And he deserved my best. He deserved the optimistic Sarah. Not the stressed-out, frantic-with-worry Sarah.

"Anyway." I glanced up at Julia. "Tell me I'm wrong to have a crumb of doubt. He's wonderful, right?"

"Let's see," Julia started. "He's cute. Nice eyes. And I like the way he studies you. Did you see how he handed you the pepper before you even asked for him to pass it?"

"You noticed that?" I smiled. "He *is* sweet."

"So—" Julia folded her linen napkin—"how involved are you two?" She leaned closer and lowered her voice. "I mean, do you think he's *The One?*"

The One . . . shorthand for the-first-guy-Sarah-Reeves-has-sex-with. To be completely honest, I've never done it.

Julia knows it. And Bailey, well, he sure knows it. Sometimes I think the entire Bay Area is aware of my virgin status. You know how the heroine in *The*

Scarlet Letter wore that "A" on her dress? Well, my letter is a "V," and sometimes I feel like it's tattooed on my forehead.

"I don't know," I said. "Not that I'm not dying to leave the world of virginity behind. It's just that— how can I be sure? I mean, David is really pushing for it. Pouring on the pressure. And I want it. But I also want to be absolutely sure that it's right."

I shook my head. "I'm rambling again. I must sound like a lunatic."

"You sound like someone with a lot of stress in her life." Julia used that thoughtful, level voice of hers. It reminded me why she was such a good friend. Julia has this incredible gift for giving you advice and space at the same time. It's like she can help you find your way through a maze from outside it.

"Think about it, Sarah," Julia added. "You've changed your entire life in the space of . . . what? A few months? There's Berkeley, and—and freshman year at college is supposed to be the hardest. You've got a new apartment. You've started off on your own—really on your own—with no financial support, no family."

"I wish I had a choice," I muttered.

Julia frowned. "Have you ever thought about calling them?" she asked quietly. "Your parents, I mean. I'm sure they'd be relieved to hear your voice . . . to find out that you're okay. And you know they want to help. They always promised to pay for college."

"Have you already forgotten what they did to Bailey?" I asked. My throat felt tight just thinking about it.

"Have *you* forgotten Bailey brought some of that trouble on himself?" Julia asked.

"Okay, but after he made amends? After he straightened out his life, they wouldn't let it go. Remember that courtroom? They prosecuted him. They tried to turn me against him. . . ."

It still hurt to remember those days. My parents didn't care at all about how I felt. They went ahead with the case, even though they knew it was ripping me up.

"And it's not only about Bailey. I can't forget about the whole adoption thing. They lied to me, Jul. For my whole life." My voice cracked a little. "I don't want to ask them for anything."

"God, I can hear the stress in your voice." Julia reached out and touched my arm. "You remind me of that Roman god Atlas. You know, the one carrying the world on his shoulders?"

"My hero," I muttered.

"Just remember, you don't have to be like that, you don't have to handle everything all alone," Julia told me.

"I'm not so sure about that," I said. Julia could go to her brothers and sister for support. She had a family. Yeah, they had fights, but they were there for each other, no matter what. No one in Julia's family would treat her the way my parents treated me.

I would not ask them for help.

I would pay my way. My rent. My car insurance. College fees and textbooks.

And I was going to do it on my own.

Or not at all.

Chapter 3

David's car is . . . wow," Bailey raved as he and David returned to the table.

I knew bringing up the car was a good idea. One trip out to the parking lot, and Bailey was treating David like one of his best buds.

It may sound sexist, but there's no denying that guys have this way of slipping into another "guy" language. They can be talking about football or cars or power tools—whatever the subject, they sort of click into the lingo, rib each other, try to impress each other and—*wham!*—they've made this connection.

They've *bonded*. I could only imagine the fuel-injected terms that had been slung around the parking lot while they drooled over David's car.

The waitress moved toward us, searching our faces for a clue as to who should get the check. It was sort of an awkward moment. The café isn't pricey, but Bailey

and I are both broke, and lately money has been tight
for Julia and her husband, Griffin, too. Deciding that
we would just have to split the bill, I reached for the
leather folder.

"This one's mine." David took the bill from the
waitress.

"You sure?" Bailey asked. "'Cause we can split it
four ways."

"No, I got it," David said casually.

"The next one's on us—at Salinger's," Bailey
promised, checking his watch. "Where I should have
been about an hour ago." Salingers is a restaurant
that's become sort of a family business for Bailey and
his older brother, Charlie.

"I'm sure they'll survive without you for a few more
minutes," Julia teased. "Anybody need a ride toward
Pacific Heights? It's my night to watch Owen."

"I'd like to stay and grab some coffee," David
hinted. He slid closer to me on the banquette.

I nodded, unable to control the urge to smile. I was
kind of pleased that David had picked up the check.
It's not as if money is the only important thing to me.
But I thought it showed that David wanted to do
something nice for my friends.

Julia and Bailey headed off, and David asked the
waitress to bring us two lattes. I settled back into the
booth, feeling much more relaxed. David slid his
hand onto my thigh, and I suddenly found it difficult
to remember why I had any doubts about him at all.

"This was great." I turned my face up to David's.
"You were great."

"Oh, really?" David sat up a little straighter. "Was
that like a test or an audition or something?"

"No," I stammered. "Not really. I mean, I did want my friends to like you. It's always a little awkward, don't you think?"

"Mmm." He leaned close, his lips just inches away from mine. "You know, you're sexy when you're nervous."

"Really?" The word squeaked out—about as sexy as a cartoon mouse.

"Yeah. The way you sway back and forth. And then start talking about nothing, just talk to fill the space. There's a sort of desperation that . . . I don't know. I like it," he teased.

"I'm glad. I mean, that's good, I guess." He was so close that I could smell a mixture of shaving cream and soap. I wanted to reach up and touch the smooth, warm skin of his jaw.

As if he could read my mind, he lifted my hand to his lips, kissed my fingertips, then pressed them to his cheek.

"Do you know what?" I babbled. "I was thinking that—"

The words were lost when David leaned down and kissed me.

Whoa. It really took my breath away.

I closed my eyes, wanting to save the moment, to wrap it in a tiny package and keep it forever.

When David held me close, there was definitely magic between us—sort of like a spark of electricity. It was one of the few bright spots in my life, probably the only good thing going for me right now.

David ended the kiss, keeping his face close to mine. "One more kiss like that and we're going to get booted out of here."

"I know what you mean." I practically purred.

The waitress came over, placed the lattes on our table without making eye contact, and hurried away.

"Wow," I said, "talk about discreet."

"It's a French café," David pointed out. "The French invented discretion. How about we finish our coffee and head over to your place?"

I was tempted to say yes. Bailey would be at work, and at the moment I wanted nothing more than to get closer to David.

Then I thought about the reality of it. A mound of dirty dishes filled the sink. Bailey had forgotten that it was his turn to vacuum and dust. My bed was covered with stacks of sheet music I'd been sorting out for the band I sing with. And I still wasn't absolutely, absolutely sure. . . .

"I don't know—" I took a sip from the bowl-shaped cup, buying time. "Everything's such a mess."

"Everything? As in your life—or as in your apartment?" David asked.

I laughed. "I was talking about my apartment, but now that you mention it, my life is a disaster area too."

"What's wrong?" he asked.

"Nothing really," I lied. I reminded myself that I didn't want all the negative stuff I was going through to infect my relationship with David.

"So why don't I come over? We can kick back. Have some time alone." He tucked a lock of my hair behind my ear, and I felt a little shiver go through me. A nice kind of shiver.

A shiver that made me think David could very well be The One. But I didn't think tonight was The Night.

I just wasn't . . . ready. So it looked like I would be wearing my "V" a little while longer at least.

"Another night, okay?" I asked.

David pulled out his credit card and tossed it on top of the bill. "Let's get out of here," he said. His voice was flat. Not cold exactly. But I could tell he was *not* happy.

"Don't be upset," I told him.

"I don't know, Sarah. You're going to give me a complex. How much rejection can a guy take?"

Was that a flicker of pain in his amber eyes? Maybe David felt things more deeply than I realized.

"It's not rejection." I reached out and covered his hand. "It's just a . . . a decision to make things really, really right for us. My apartment is a mess. Dusty and—yuck! And I have this thing, this idea. Maybe it's corny and romantic. But when we're together for the first time, I want things to be perfect. I want lacy sheets and beautiful music. And . . . and fresh flowers like, everywhere."

David frowned.

"I'm sorry," I said.

"Don't be." He squeezed my knee and smiled. "You should have exactly what you want. And I'm going to make sure that you get it."

I studied his face. "You think I'm nuts."

"Not at all. Should I book the Botanical Gardens?" He plucked a rose out of the vase on the table and handed it to me.

I laughed. "Overkill."

"Okay. But don't be surprised when I knock on your door with . . . what was it? Lace sheets. A couple of CDs. And a truck full of flowers."

"Oh, come on," I waved him off.

"I promise you, it's going to happen, Sarah." At that moment, there was no mistaking the intent in his smoky eyes. David was serious. He really wanted to be with me—and he was going to do whatever it took to make it happen. I was flattered—and a little nervous.

David leaned forward and nearly stole my breath away with a sudden deep kiss. "The next time I come knocking on your door, you won't have any more excuses."

I stepped out of the shower the next morning—and the doorbell rang. Was I crazy to assume that it was David making good on his promise?

"Oh, great." I tugged on my terry-cloth robe and wrapped a towel around my head. I faced the steamy bathroom mirror and stared at my reflection. One look at me in this getup and David would burst into uncontrollable laughter.

Is it any wonder that I've begun to believe that that perfect romantic moment is never going to happen for me?

The doorbell rang again. Relentless. Determined.

David was not going to go away.

I trudged toward the door, making up funny excuses in my head. Things like: *Sarah is off at school; I'm her evil twin, Serena.* Or: *I've decided that people don't wear enough terry cloth.*

Again, the doorbell.

I twisted the knob and pulled the door open. "Okay, David," I began. "You're nothing if not—"

"Sarah . . . ?"

It wasn't David.

It was a woman.

The air seemed to rush out of my lungs as I recognized her.

She was thin and graceful, with vibrant brown eyes. Eyes like mine.

It was—my mother.

Chapter 4

My birth mother. The one who pulled the disappearing act. The absolute last person I expected to see standing outside my door.

So much for my clean break.

I blinked, wishing that I could make the woman before me disappear as easily as I'd ripped up all those letters I wrote her. No such luck.

"Mind if I come in?" Robin asked.

I couldn't speak. I cautiously backed away from the open door and crossed the room. She followed me inside, closing the door quietly behind her.

"I guess you're surprised to see me," she started to say.

I perched on the arm of the worn sofa and crossed my arms in front of me. "Surprised?" I repeated. "Yeah. Maybe a little. I mean, I was kind of expecting you—oh, I don't know—two years ago?"

She clenched her eyes shut for a moment, as if hit by a wave of pain.

So she looks upset. So what? I thought. She's an actress.

"I deserved that," Robin admitted.

"Maybe. Maybe not. It's not like you owed me anything," I answered. "You gave me away when I was born—end of commitment. I don't know why I expected anything from you."

"You have every reason to be angry," she told me. "Before the tour, when we met, I had so much hope for us. We were becoming friends, Sarah. After so many years, we'd gotten this chance to make a connection. And it was a good thing."

"Was it? Was it really?" My face grew hot as tears formed in my eyes. "Because after you left, after I wrote a half-dozen letters that you never answered, I began to wonder. Maybe I should never have contacted you. Maybe it would have been better not to have met you at all."

"Sarah, please . . ." She touched my shoulder, but I pulled away.

"Because if I'd never met you, I could have held on to the dream . . . that ridiculous, naive dream that adopted kids have. You know, like, my real parents really wanted me. That they wanted me and were looking everywhere, but just couldn't find me," I explained. I forced myself to look right at her, meeting her gaze.

I couldn't tell her the whole thing, how I had this dream once that my mother was this beautiful queen and my father was this fair, loving king. That they loved me, but this horrible ogre stole me away.

Sounds cheesy, I know. But when you're adopted, you need to fill in the blank spaces from your past.

Tears were streaming down my cheeks, and I wiped at them with the backs of my hands.

"Oh, Sarah, I am sorry." Robin's face was pinched with sadness. I saw sympathy in her eyes.

But she's an *actress,* I reminded myself again. I couldn't forget that. I wasn't going to let Robin fool me into thinking she cared about me. Not this time.

I sank onto the couch. The rush of emotion had taken me by surprise, and suddenly I felt drained.

"I should have gotten in touch," she admitted. "I could have called or written. But I'm a horrible writer. My letters make good bedtime reading. They're full of boring details, guaranteed to put you to sleep."

She smiled. I didn't. It was such a lame excuse. Like I would care if her letters were boring. If she'd written anything, anything at all, at least I would have known she was thinking about me.

"Oh, Sarah. This is so hard." Robin cleared her throat. "We planned to do this together. Me and Jeremy. He was going to help me explain."

I blinked. Who was she talking about? "My—my father?" I asked.

"No. He was . . . he and I didn't have a great relationship. I'm talking about my husband. Jeremy," Robin explained.

"Your husband?" I looked up at her. "You got married?" I didn't know anything about her, I realized. She was my *mother* and I didn't even know she got married.

"In Canada. Toronto. It was sort of a spur-of-the-moment decision, but it turned out to be one of the best choices I've ever made." A smile broke across Robin's face.

Was she expecting me to be happy for her or something?

"So . . . that accounts for, like, maybe two weeks of the time you've been away. What about the rest?" I asked. The answer came to me in a flash. "Oh, I get it. You were afraid to tell this Jeremy the details of your past. You didn't want him to know you'd had a kid, right?"

"No. That's not it at all." Her eyes glistened with tears. "Jeremy heard about you all the time. Nearly every day."

I frowned. "That must have made for fascinating conversation." I paused. "So now what? You're here to parade me around? You want me to meet him, is that it?"

"I . . . you can't meet him, Sarah." Robin swallowed hard. "He . . . he died."

Chapter 5

I stopped cold. Robin's husband had *died?* What could I possibly say now?

"What happened?" I asked quietly.

"A car accident. He was traveling for business, but . . ." Her voice trailed off.

For the first time since she walked into the apartment, I really looked at Robin. She'd lost weight. Her clothes were a little baggy, and she appeared too skinny to be healthy.

The skin under her eyes was creased and gray, and her cheeks were pale. She looked like someone who'd gone through a lot. Jeremy's death had taken its toll.

"I'm sorry." Robin gathered herself. "It was a mistake to come here. I shouldn't have bothered you."

"No," I protested, rising from the sofa. "I mean . . .

don't say that." I buried my hands in the pockets of my bathrobe, pacing nervously.

I felt bad for Robin. I did. But the fact that her husband died didn't wipe away all the pain she'd caused me. I couldn't just forgive her because she'd been through a really hard time. But I couldn't throw her out either.

"Look, I'd better get going." Robin headed toward the door. "I caught you at a bad time. You just got out of the shower."

"I have a class," I told her.

"You must be . . ." Her eyes were thoughtful as she calculated. "In college now?"

At least she remembered my age. "I'm a freshman at Berkeley."

"Berkeley? Fantastic." She tried to sound enthusiastic, but I could tell it was hard for her to switch gears. She picked up a pen and jotted something down on the notepad by the phone. "Here's my number. Call me if you . . . well, I'd like to hear from you, but . . ."

I was still trying to figure out what to say to her when she rushed out the door and shut it behind her.

After class I was a wreck. I had to talk to somebody. I needed to go over every detail of what had happened between me and Robin—from the moment she rang the doorbell to the moment she gave me her number and ran out.

If David and I were closer, I would have gone to him. But we were still in "early dating" mode. And David didn't know about Robin. He didn't even know that I was adopted. It's just not one of those things that you spring on someone between "Nice weather" and "Let's see a movie."

I decided to head home and talk it out with Bailey. He was the perfect person. Who knew more about this whole situation than my former boyfriend Bay? He helped me find Robin in the first place. I made a beeline for the apartment.

Unfortunately, it was dark and empty.

"Bailey?" I called, peering into his empty room.

Big surprise—he wasn't home.

Bailey spent loads of time helping his big brother, Charlie, out at home. If he wasn't with his brothers and sisters, he was working at Salingers. And if he wasn't at home or at Salinger's, he was at one of his AA meetings.

Wow, in the same week I ate Chinese food with him *and* went to that French café with him, Julia, and David. I must have used up my Bailey time for at least a month already.

There was no way I was spending the afternoon sitting in our apartment all by myself. I would go nuts with all these mixed-up thoughts about Robin racing through my head. I needed to talk them out to make sense of them.

I jumped in the car and drove over to the Coffeehouse. Julia liked to hang out there and write in her journal. But when I checked inside, I didn't see one familiar face.

I drove past the Salingers' Victorian-style house, but Julia's car was gone. Julia is almost as busy as Bailey lately. She was probably at the grocery store. Or picking Owen up from day care. Or taking Claudia somewhere. Ever since the time Charlie got sick, Julia started doing a lot of extra family-type stuff. Plus she had a part-time job working for a professor.

There must be someone else I can talk to, I thought as I started back home. It's not like Bailey and Julia were my *only* friends, right?

Except, actually, right now they sort of were. I was in this weird between-friends stage. A lot of my high school friends had gone to college out of state. I met some cool people in my classes, but nobody that I felt super close to. And you have to feel really close to someone if you're going to spill your guts to them.

You're in this alone, I thought. *Sure, Bailey and Julia care about you. But they have their own lives. They aren't always going to be able to be there for you.*

Right then, all I wanted was to talk to my mother— my adoptive mother. The woman I'd thought of as my mom for most of my life. I wanted to sit at the kitchen table and tell her everything, the way I had so many times before.

But I couldn't do that. I hadn't been home since I moved out. And I hadn't had a real conversation with my mom, you know, one of those real heart-to-heart ones, since I found out I was adopted. After that I didn't feel like I could really trust her anymore.

I turned onto my street and drove straight by my apartment. I decided to stop by Salingers instead. There was a decent chance Bailey would be there. And if he wasn't, well, I'd think about that later.

Fortunately, I found Bailey at the restaurant, covering the early shift.

"Hey!" I waved at him from the bar area. "There you are!"

He carried a tray of clean glasses behind the bar.

"Whoa! Sarah! I wasn't expecting you to be here." He paused, frowning. "Wait a minute. Did we plan to do something today? Oh, man. Sarah, I'm sorry—"

I smiled and shook my head. Same old Bay. "Relax, you didn't forget any plans. It's just that . . . I need to talk."

"Oh. Well, okay. What's up?" Bailey prompted me.

I took a deep breath. "She's back in town. My real mother." Quickly, I filled in the details of that morning.

"Wow. Robin is back." Bailey slid a clear wineglass upside down into the rack over our heads. "So—that's good, right?"

"I don't know, Bailey. That's the problem." I struggled to explain. "At first I *counted* on her coming back. Then, when she didn't, I sort of wrote her out of my life. She's the one who let me down—twice! So now that she's reappeared, what am I supposed to do? Be happy about it?"

He nodded. "You've got a point."

"On the other hand, if I never call her, if I just pretend she never showed up, doesn't that make me just like *her?* Carrying on the rejection thing forever?"

"So—you're going to give her another shot?" Bailey asked.

I climbed onto a barstool and covered my eyes with my hands. "I don't know." I'd reached a total dead end. "The thing that scares me is—"

"Bailey!" called a voice from the kitchen. "The chef needs a minute."

"Hold that thought," Bailey said, turning toward the kitchen door. "I'll be right back."

He disappeared, leaving me sitting alone, feeling sort of—well—foolish. I could feel the eyes of the early-dinner crowd on me—wondering about that poor girl sitting at the bar—alone.

"What am I doing here?" I muttered to myself.

"Sarah . . ." Bailey rushed out the kitchen door and touched my shoulder. "Give me two seconds. I just have to change the dinner specials." He hurried into the dining room.

I waited, tapping my fingers on the bar.

A waiter walked by and gave me a curious look. Suddenly I wondered if the staff thought I was some loser, a royal pain in the neck who did nothing but bother Bailey.

"Okay, okay," Bailey said breathlessly as he returned. "So . . . we were talking about Robin."

"Salinger," the waiter said. "Table six wants to talk with you. Personally."

"In a minute," he told the waiter.

I slid off the barstool. This was a waste of time. Bailey meant well, but there was no way he could squeeze in a thoughtful conversation while managing the restaurant. I was going to have to deal with this alone.

"Look," I said, "you're busy. And I probably need to work this out on my own anyway. I don't know why I'm making such a big deal out of it. I mean, she was my mother for a couple of days. Why should I care? Why make a big deal out of that now?" I stared out of the restaurant.

"Because—" Bailey stopped me. "Because she's your *mother.*" His blue eyes were pensive, studying me. "Even if she didn't raise you, she *is* your mother. And she's here now. And—and I'd give anything to have my mother here—to have the chance you have, Sarah. Think about it."

"Bailey, there's someone on the phone who wants to know if they can book the restaurant for a private party," the hostess called.

"Go on. It's okay. Really," I told him.

"Listen, I promised Owen I'd do this finger-painting thing with him tonight, but maybe after that we can talk more," Bailey volunteered. Then he picked up the phone behind the bar.

"Bye," I whispered.

It was obvious I was going to have to figure this one out on my own.

And I had no idea what I should do.

Chapter 6

So I did the only thing I could think of. I called Robin. I had a long conversation with myself, and then I called her.

I was feeling really, really alone—and there she was, wanting to spend time with me. Calling her seemed like the right thing to do.

But I didn't plan to let her get too close. I wasn't going to let her hurt me again. I agreed to meet her for lunch. Lunch seemed safe.

That's how I ended up sitting across from Robin in the Fog City Diner, this cool restaurant just across the Embarcadero from the bay. So far we'd been keeping the things light. If you looked up the word "chitchat" in the dictionary, you'd probably see a transcript of our conversation.

And that was fine with me. I didn't want to get into anything personal with Robin. If she walked away again, I would feel as if I lost a casual acquaintance, not a mother. At least that's what I kept telling myself.

"And that was my earliest memory of the bay." Robin finished her story. "The day my parents took me on the ferry to Sausalito." She stabbed a cherry tomato with her fork and wrinkled her nose. "Can't we talk about you? How's school? And what about your band? Is the Nielsen Family still together?"

Whoa. She remembered the name of the band. Maybe she wasn't lying when she said she and her husband used to talk about me a lot.

Don't get all emotional, I told myself. Chitchat. That's all you're doing today.

"We have a gig in a few weeks, singing at a festival," I answered. "And school is great. Sometimes, when I walk around the campus, I have to pinch myself to believe it's real. Like I don't deserve to be there."

"You've worked hard for it," Robin pointed out. "Don't undermine your achievements, Sarah."

I waved her off. I wasn't ready to go there. I wasn't ready to let Robin see the real Sarah—broke, struggling, lonely.

But I was curious about her past. If *Robin* was the one telling the personal stuff, that would be okay.

"So you grew up in San Francisco. Is your family still here?" I asked.

The smile faded from Robin's face. "No. My parents are gone."

I had to ask. I mean, her family was my family too. "Did they move away? Or are they—?"

"My parents are dead," she said quietly. "For just about twenty years now."

"Oh." I looked down at the shiny spoon by my plate. "I'm sorry." My grandparents were gone. It was weird, but I felt disappointed. I would never have a chance to meet them.

Robin fiddled with her napkin. She seemed upset. It was obviously still hard for her to talk about her parents' death, even though they died twenty years ago.

Wait. Twenty years ago? Did Robin's parents die around the time that she was pregnant . . . with me?

"How about dessert?" Robin changed the subject. "They have a killer cheesecake here."

I hesitated. I wasn't sure it was a great idea to spend more time with Robin right now. I wanted to take things really slow. But I was kind of curious. There was so much I didn't know about my own family. I didn't even know the names of my grandparents.

"Dessert sounds great," I told her. "But you've got to try San Francisco's best-kept secret."

"What's that? A new flavor of ice cream?" Robin asked.

I smiled. "No, it's this little pastry shop in North Beach. I'll take you there, only you have to promise not to disclose the location to unworthy individuals."

She put a credit card on the bill and handed it to our waiter. She leaned across the table. "How do you know *I'm* worthy?"

That's the question of the day, I thought. But I just shrugged.

We headed out of the diner. The air was windy and cool and refreshing, so we decided to walk to North Beach. When we passed the foot of Telegraph Hill, I got an idea.

"Why don't we hike up Coit Tower?" I suggested. "It's a climb, but you feel totally proud of yourself when you get to the top!"

"Been there, done that," Robin said. "I used to date a guy who knew every makeout spot on Telegraph Hill."

"Really?" I laughed.

"Uh-huh. But I'm not up for a climb today," she answered. "Let's just stroll and soak in the sunlight."

As we walked, I had to restrain myself from firing questions off at Robin. Now that she'd given me a small bit of information about my family, my curiosity was piqued.

But if I started asking a bunch of questions, Robin might think it was okay to ask a lot of personal stuff about me. And it wasn't. At least not yet.

We found a small round table at the Patisserie, where we split a rich, flaky pastry. I let Robin do most of the talking. She told one funny story after the next. Once she'd nearly stopped a performance at the opera with a loud sneeze. Another time her parents had been livid when she'd gotten stuck at Alcatraz after the last ferry had left.

I tried to decide what I'd think of Robin if she were someone I was meeting for the first time. There were some women around her age in a few of my classes. If Robin were one of them, and we were just hanging out, having dessert, would I be having a good time? Would she be someone I'd want to spend more time with?

Yes, I decided. Robin was funny and smart. And she was actually pretty *comfortable*. I could see just kicking back with her, watching TV or something. Or at least I could see it if we didn't have all this history between us.

As we left the café, Robin glanced down the street

and grinned. "There *is* something from my childhood that I still like to do," she began to say.

"Walk across the Golden Gate Bridge?" I asked.

She shook her head. "Bridges make my knees shake."

"Tea in the Japanese Garden?" I guessed again.

"Sounds nice," Robin said. "But I was thinking in a wilder vein." The clang of a cable car sounded, and she pointed down the street.

"You are kidding me!" When she shook her head, I let out a scream. "I love cable cars."

"Well, come on, before we miss it."

We raced down the block, chasing the car as it neared a stop. I was out of breath by the time we squeezed into the crowd and stepped on. Robin was huffing and puffing too.

Sometimes when I'm feeling really confused and lousy, I go for the cheapest therapy San Francisco has to offer—a ride on a cable car. Lurching down the city's steepest hills—it can really make you reevaluate your life. Probably because you're so scared, it flashes before your eyes.

There's a certain way you have to move toward the car as it pauses, quickly wedge yourself in, then hold on for dear life.

Robin was a pro.

"Now I know how the inside of a peanut butter sandwich feels," I called out to Robin.

She laughed, and nodded toward the corner. "Next stop? That will put me right by the BART station. I should really catch the next train to my place."

The car slowed and we jumped off onto the cobblestone street. "I've got to go too," I told her. David and I had plans later on.

We stared at each other for a moment. I didn't know exactly what to say. It's not like I could just say "see ya" and wander off. We might have kept our conversation pretty light. But today was a big deal—for both of us.

"Well, um, lunch was great," I thanked her. It sounded totally lame.

"Jeez, this entire afternoon has been sort of the biography of Robin," she observed. "What's that joke? 'Enough about me. What do *you* think about me?'"

That's exactly the way I wanted it, I thought.

"That's okay," I answered.

"It's not okay with me," Robin pressed on. "I had so many things I wanted to ask you. Did you get what you wanted for Christmas the year you were five? Who was your best friend in high school? I spent so much time wondering about you. Worrying about whether you were safe and healthy and happy."

"Did you—did you really?" I stared at the ground, unable to look at her face. I didn't want her to see that my eyes were wet with tears.

How did the conversation get so personal? What happened to chitchat?

Robin touched my shoulder, then let her hand fall away. "And now I look at you and you're so beautiful and smart and perfect. All that worrying for nothing!" she said with a laugh. "You are so . . . *together.*"

"Ha!" I snickered. I blinked the tears away. "Got you fooled."

"Hardly," Robin insisted. "I can't take credit for it, but I am proud. Proud to know such a bright, talented person. That you can even find time to sing with the band while you're at Berkeley . . . you really do it all.

If you had met me when I was your age?" She groaned. "There's no comparison. You are so much more together, Sarah."

It's not true! I wanted to say. It made me cringe to hear her telling me how proud she was. Because she didn't know me at all. My life was a mess. I was broke, struggling to figure out exactly what I wanted my relationship with David to be, feeling so alone sometimes.

Part of me wanted to spill my troubles right then and there. But who was I kidding? Robin was a stranger. And I wasn't one of those people who felt comfortable advertising their personal life to strangers.

So I just flashed her a smile and pretended that everything was fine.

What I always do. Typical Sarah.

Sometimes it's hard to be the eternal optimist.

Chapter 7

Passion? You picked a movie called *Passion?*"

"Subtle, huh?" David held my hand and led the way toward the door. "And I already bought our tickets."

"Let's just hope it's good," I warned him. "Or you are dead meat."

Fortunately, it wasn't the drippy romance the title suggested. The film was in French with English subtitles, and it was a comedy about four people who keep falling in love with the wrong person. By the time it was over, I felt relaxed and giddy from laughing so hard.

I bet Robin would like it. I have to remember to tell her about it, I thought.

That was happening more and more often. I'd be doing something and Robin would pop into my mind. I'd seen her a bunch of times the past few weeks.

I kept telling myself I shouldn't say yes every time she suggested getting together. But Robin could be really convincing. I'd start out saying "I'm not sure" and end up saying "I'll meet you there." And you know what? I was having fun.

Robin was becoming a friend. And I really needed a friend right now. Especially because Bailey and Julia were always so busy.

I kept reminding myself that she'd been back in my life only a few weeks—and that she could just walk right out anytime. I absolutely could not forget that.

"You're way quieter than usual," David noticed as he walked me home.

"Just thinking," I told him.

"About *Passion?*" he teased.

"Uh, not really," I answered.

We climbed up the steps to my apartment building. "The temperature must have dropped. How about some tea?" I asked without really thinking about it first.

"Sure." David followed me into my apartment. He shrugged off his coat and picked out a CD while I turned on the burner under the kettle.

"I think we have some cookies." I peered into the cabinet. "Hmm. Guess not. Bailey strikes again."

"That's okay." David stepped into the kitchen. He dropped his hands onto my shoulders and gently tilted his face down toward mine. "You're sweet enough."

I gave an exaggerated wince. "Ugh! What a line," I complained.

"Corny, but true." He leaned down and brushed his lips over mine. I closed my eyes and slid my hands over his shoulders. It felt good to be in David's arms. Warm, exciting, even a little dangerous.

Because I knew where a kiss could lead.

I rested my head against his chest, and for a moment we swayed together, doing this sort of slow dance in the kitchen.

It's now or never, I thought.

David leaned back. One of his warm hands rested against my cheek. "Do you want to—?"

I nodded. "In my bedroom . . ." As I took his hand and led him down the hall, I felt a little twinge of . . . something. Just a feeling of something being a little off.

I was a grown woman. I was entitled to make this choice. I would be careful and responsible. So why was that tiny needle of guilt suddenly stabbing at my conscience?

"Don't look so guilty." David sat down beside me on the bed. "It's not like we're in high school and your parents are going to catch us."

"That's true," I admitted. But his words bothered me. Because I felt like I didn't have any parents. Or maybe I had three. But David didn't know that. There were a lot of things that David didn't know about me.

"Don't be nervous," he whispered. His fingers moved up my arms, making little circles on my shoulders. Suddenly, I felt incredibly ticklish. I clasped my hand down over his, blocking the motion.

"What is it? What's wrong?" David sounded concerned. But I caught a faint trace of annoyance in his tone too.

"I don't know. It's just that . . . You're tickling me." I decided to give the easy explanation.

"Oh. Sorry." He slid his hands behind my back and

42

pulled me closer. "We can't have you laughing. This is serious stuff."

I tried to kiss him again, but somehow the mood had vanished. As I pressed closer to him, I found myself wondering why I *couldn't* laugh. I mean, didn't David realize that I love jokes? No, he didn't. He didn't know much about me at all. He didn't know about my financial problems, or my family problems or my favorite color. David saw just a tiny facet of my life—Sarah, the girl who was upbeat and studious, the girl who agreed to be his project partner in Criminal Justice 101.

"Just relax," he whispered, massaging my shoulder. "I can feel all this tension in your muscles."

"David," I began. "I can't do this."

"Sure you can," he insisted. "You just need to—"

The kettle whistled. Yes! The perfect excuse to spring off the bed! I dashed into the kitchen, turned off the stove, and took a deep breath.

You know what to do, I told myself. *Follow your instincts. Don't take this step until you are absolutely ready.*

I was trying to figure out what to say to David, when I heard his footsteps behind me. He was in the living room, pulling on his coat.

"David? You don't have to leave," I said. "I mean, okay, I'm not ready to . . . to . . ."

"Don't bother explaining," he snapped. "This is a waste of time. Why am I even here?"

"David, wait," I said. "It's just that everything is happening too soon. We need to get to know each other better."

"Save it. I got the message." He popped the bolt and threw open the door. "I'm out of here."

"David—" I stepped toward him, but before I could say anything, he stepped out, slamming the door behind him.

You know the worst thing about that night?

After David left, I had no one to talk to. Julia was out with Griffin, and Bailey was, you guessed it, at the restaurant.

This was definitely one of those situations that needed to be analyzed. Did I totally mess up? What should I have said to David? I wasn't in the kitchen *that* long. Why did he just assume I wasn't coming back?

Suddenly I understood why people called those radio talk shows. I really needed to have a marathon conversation with someone right now. But I was totally on my own.

Well, I could call Robin. . . . But I wasn't up for having a big heart-to-heart with her. Not yet. Not until I was sure she wasn't going to pull another disappearing act on me.

I changed into my bathrobe and brushed out my hair and tried to figure out what I had done wrong. I had tried so hard with David. I mean, I didn't talk about all my problems. I didn't complain. I was the usual optimistic Sarah almost all the time. So what was the problem?

"Face it," I told myself, slumping onto the couch. "You're just defective. Not good girlfriend material."

Hours later, I was sitting on the sofa and clutching a mug of hot chocolate—and still thinking about David—when Bailey stopped in.

"Hey." He grinned, all dimples. "I just wanted to grab a clean shirt. Then I'm heading out for the night.

I probably won't see you till—whoa. What happened to you?"

"Does it show?" I muttered.

"Okay. Either you had a bad day, or you're auditioning for the role of Grumpy in *Snow White.*"

I smiled. Bailey has a way of cutting to the chase. "Call me Grumpy. Call me Virgin. Call me Hopeless."

"Oh." Bailey knew exactly where I was coming from. He'd been there with me before. He sat down on the arm of the sofa and listened intently as I recapped my date with David.

"God, I feel like such a loser. I can't even stay in a relationship with a guy long enough to have sex. I feel like I have no friends, even though I know it's not really true. I don't ever talk to two of my parents. And I'm not sure I can trust the one I *do* talk to."

I took a deep breath and kept talking. Bailey didn't say a word. He's a guy who knows when to listen.

"I'm so broke that even if I eat peanut butter sandwiches like *every day,* I still may not be able to scrape up money for next semester—and registration is in a couple of days," I rushed on. "I'm going to end up dropping out and working as a french fry girl someplace."

"Not so bad. Those little hats french fry girls wear would look really sexy on you," Bailey teased.

I gave a strangled laugh.

Bailey raked his hands through his hair. "You're upset about this thing with David, so it's making the whole world look horrible to you. It's like you're depressed about one thing—and the feeling sort of, I don't know, takes over. And then you're depressed about everything."

I took a sip of my hot chocolate. "Maybe . . ."

"No. I think that's it. Really. I know the whole—virginity thing—gets to you." Bailey suddenly seemed interested in a dirty glass sitting on the floor. He stared at it as he spoke. "But when you want it, it's going to happen for you. Definitely."

"I just wish I didn't feel so out of control right now," I answered.

"Hey, if anyone can pull things together, Sarah, it's you." He got up from the arm of the sofa and headed for the door. "I mean, if someone asked me who is the most together girl in the world, I'd say Sarah Reeves. Hands down." He smiled and left. The door slammed shut behind him.

Bailey thought I was together. Julia thought I was an optimist. Robin thought I had accomplished so much.

But I was falling, drowning, letting everything in my life turn into a complete ruin. And no one knew!

I, Sarah Reeves, was a total fraud.

Chapter 8

"Sarah, I'm sorry. I'm like, really late for a party," Justin apologized.

I don't know why I decided to call Justin. I mean, he's going to school on the East Coast. *Many* time zones away.

I guess it was because, so far, this weekend felt like the longest, loneliest one of my life. Bailey was working round-the-clock at Salingers. Julia was in Los Angeles, where Claudia was performing at a violin competition. And I wasn't about to call David—I didn't know what I wanted to say to him yet.

Anyway, I started flipping through my address book. I saw Justin's name, and just dialed. We were good friends in high school. And I could use a good friend right now.

"Hey," I teased. "I thought the curriculum was supposed to be tough there."

"Listen, even Yalies need to let off some steam every now and then. So . . ." he said. "Can I call you back? Maybe next week, after midterms?"

"Next week? Sure," I said casually. What else could I say? *Please stay on the line! I'm running out of friends, and I'm starting to feel desperate!* Not something you do to someone on the other end of the continent. "Later, Justin."

I hung up the phone. I thought about calling Robin. But I liked to let her be the one to call *me.* I wasn't ready to start assuming she'd be there when I needed her. If she wanted to call—and she did call a lot—fine. If she didn't, that was fine too.

I was pretty glad when Monday finally rolled around. At least at registration I'd be around *people.* Strangers, sure, but still warm, living human beings.

Maybe a few too many of them. Berkeley's massive registration hall was already packed when I arrived.

Freshman registration is one of those nightmares of university life. Since freshmen are the last to register, we usually get closed out of the best classes. And *we're* the only ones who have to do *arena* registration. Everyone else gets to type their class choices into a computer.

I carefully navigated around two guys who actually lugged their bikes into the hall. I heard a familiar voice behind me.

"Okay, so, you hate me."

I turned and glanced up at David. His bangs were still wet from a shower, and a little stubble shadowed his square jaw.

Ooh. I couldn't help thinking. *Definitely a hottie.*

"I know. You think I'm a total creep," he added.

"I never said that," I told him.

"But you were thinking it."

"And now you're a mind reader?" I teased. "This is why people do not date psych majors. One class on Freud and you guys start jumping into everybody's brain."

"I'm sorry," he told me. "About the other night, not about Freud. Come to think of it, I apologize for Freud too. He's a little loony."

I laughed. "Well, there go a hundred years of psychotherapy."

David smiled. "Now, that's the Sarah I know."

Our eyes met, and I took a breath. Yeah, that's the Sarah *he* knew. Cheerful, carefree. The problem was, he didn't know the real me.

"David, I know the other night was . . . well, pretty awful, but . . ." I began.

"Don't. Just . . . don't." He shook his head. "I don't want to rehash the whole thing."

"No. I want to explain," I told him.

I realized I had to stop pretending. If I was going to get close to David, then I had to let him *see* me. I couldn't blame him for not knowing the important stuff if I never told him any of it.

"The thing is, I've been going through a lot recently," I continued. "There's this thing with my parents. Not the most pleasant situation—"

"Stop right there." He held his hands up.

"Huh?" I stared at him. "What do you—"

"Sarah, look. You don't owe me any explanation. I was wrong and I'm sorry. Let's just put it behind us."

He put his hands on my shoulders, his face only inches from mine as he spoke. "We have so much fun when we're together—at least we usually do. Let's not waste time with anything else."

But if it's all just fun, I thought, wouldn't that keep our relationship totally on the surface? Didn't I want something more like what I had with Bailey? I mean, we really talked to each other—and helped each other through some bad stuff.

"David, there's more to life than fun." I frowned.

"Yeah, there are papers to write, and boring jobs to go to, and hassles with families, and four hundred other kinds of garbage," David said. "But when I'm with you, I forget about all that. You're like a mini-vacation. You're like—my Bahamas."

How silly—but sweet. I couldn't stop myself from smiling.

"I want to be your vacation too. When you're with me, I don't want you to think about anything negative."

Hmm. With all the stuff going on in my life, vacation sounded kind of nice. "Okay," I said. "But before vacation, I have to go register for English."

"And I have to go to work. But I'll call you later." David turned to walk away, then stopped.

"One word of warning." He rubbed the sleeve of my velvet top. "This sweater is . . . it's a killer. If you wear it next time we're alone together, I can't be held accountable for my actions." He grinned.

"Oh, really?" I challenged.

"Really."

"In that case," I told him, "I'll never take it off."

Hey, you're *supposed* to flirt with cute guys on vacation, right?

I gave him a quick kiss and rushed over to the English table.

"Remember—think positive," he called after me.

The English line wasn't very long. I hoped that didn't mean all the good classes were already filled.

When the clerk told me I could get my first-choice class, I almost laughed.

"You're kidding me," I said.

The guy handed me the card. "We don't joke about stuff like this. But this is the last card for this class. Guard it with your life."

I smiled. Yes! I just squeaked in! Maybe my luck was changing. Or maybe David was right. Maybe all I need to do is start thinking positive.

Think positive, I repeated to myself as I waited in the long line at sociology.

Maybe the positive-energy thing really worked. Because half an hour later, I had registered for every class I wanted. Every single one. That *never* happens! I fanned the class cards out in my hand and grinned down at them.

Yes, the key is thinking positive, I decided. When you're worried all the time, that negative energy can really get out of control and affect everything in your life. I had to remember that.

Think positive. It was going to be my mantra from now on.

Whew! I felt like a huge weight had been lifted off my shoulders as I made my way back to the bursar's table to pay the registration fees.

I pulled my Visa card out of my wallet. I should have just enough credit to cover this, I thought. Berkeley is supposedly free to state residents, but fees like this added up to hundreds of dollars.

I thought about the pitiful amount of money left in my checking account. I was going to have to be so careful this semester—no movies, no takeout Chinese. Oh, well, at least my "vacation" with David was free. And I could get another job this summer and stash some money away.

I reached the front of the line, and the clerk brought my file up on the computer. She handed me an invoice for registration. Yeah, the card should just cover it.

The clerk swiped my card through the machine and put it back on the counter.

The machine beeped. The clerk frowned. "I can't accept this card," she told me. "Do you have something else?"

"What?" I asked. My voice came out in a squeak. "Why can't you use this one?"

She shrugged, not really concerned. "It says you're over your limit. So how do you want to pay?"

"What?" I was beginning to panic. All my other credit cards had been maxed out months ago.

I should have looked at my bills more closely. I always forget how fast the interest adds up. My stomach lurched.

"How do you want to pay?" the clerk repeated impatiently.

"I . . . oh, let's see." My face felt hot as I dug through my knapsack. I pulled out my checkbook and picked up a pen. "I'll write a check."

I filled in the blanks and signed my name. The room seemed to be spinning around me.

My throat felt dry and gritty as I tore off the check. Suddenly, it was hard to breathe.

This was it. This check was all the money I had left in the world.

Now I'd have no money for food. No money for rent.

Food and shelter. Necessities. Basic necessities that I couldn't afford.

The clerk reached out her hand for the check.

I bolted toward the door, my check still with me.

But no matter how fast I ran, I couldn't get away from the horrible truth.

I was out of money—flat broke.

And I couldn't afford to register for school.

Which left one option—I had to drop out.

Chapter 9

I know I'm a good risk," I told the loan officer.

This was the last bank on my list. If I didn't get a loan here . . .

"When I applied to rent my apartment, I got approval practically overnight. And . . . and . . ." I pointed to the loan application in Ms. Templeton's hands. "Did you notice that I'm attending Berkeley? My employment potential after college will be . . . like . . . really huge."

My wool skirt was itching the backs of my legs, even through my nylons. I tried not to squirm in the hard chair. I wanted to look calm, calm and super responsible.

She lowered the application to give me a stern look. I forced myself to smile back.

Ms. Templeton must think I'm a total, babbling

moron, I thought. Had I really said: *"like . . . really huge"* to a loan officer? What was I thinking?

I gripped the chair's armrests to keep my hands from shaking. The polished wooden surface of Ms. Templeton's desk gleamed up at me. So impractical. How could anyone write on that thing? How could anyone feel comfortable in a place like this, with slick marble floors, glass walls, and hushed tones?

It was totally intimidating.

"Have you considered the federally funded student loan program?" Ms. Templeton asked crisply.

"Yes, but it's too late to apply for next semester. I don't—" I swallowed hard. My throat felt so tight. "I don't want to drop out of school, Ms. Templeton."

"Of course not. But I'm afraid that we can't help you either. Ordinarily, I could sign off the paperwork. But your credit card debt is just too high." She shook her head. "You're overextended, Ms. Reeves."

"But—I pay my bills," I told her.

"Of course you do, but I'm afraid the loan is based on a simple formula. Which just doesn't work in your case."

I put my hand to my forehead, trying to focus. This couldn't be. It was my last chance. They couldn't turn me down, they just couldn't.

"Why don't I keep your application on file?" Ms. Templeton said in a gentle voice. "If your status changes, if you pay off your debts, or if you can provide collateral, we'll reconsider the loan."

I wanted to thank the woman, just to be polite, but I was afraid that my voice would crack with a sob. Instead, I stood up, gave her a quick nod, and walked out of the bank in silence.

I headed home to bury my head under my pillow. Maybe I could rack my brain for a way to come up with a few thousand dollars fast.

How had this happened?

How had I let things get so out of control?

Welcome to reality, I thought. When I walked out of my parents' house, I felt so sure of myself. So sure I could make it through four years of college without any help from them. But I was wrong. I couldn't do it on my own.

When I got home, the apartment felt dark and depressing. I wasn't sure where Bailey was—maybe off at a meeting. I called Julia, but there was no answer. I couldn't stay here alone. But what could I do? I had about twelve cents in my wallet.

I thought about grabbing my books and camping out in the Berkeley library, just to be around other people. But right now there was no way I could concentrate on studying.

I flopped down on my bed. There had to be somewhere I could go. My eyes locked on the old water bottle sitting in the corner. Yes! I jumped up and hurried over to it.

I tipped the jug over and coins spilled onto the rug. Mostly nickels and pennies. "What happened to all the quarters?" I muttered as I fished through the change.

". . . Thirty, forty, fifty . . ." I counted under my breath as I stacked coins on the counter at the Coffeehouse. The clerk waited patiently, watching without comment.

"I'm really sorry," I told him. It was embarrassing,

but this was the only way I could swing a cup of latte. At least the refills were free.

"No problem." The clerk shrugged. "I needed the nickels. Saves me from having to open up a brand-new roll." He scooped up the coins.

He must think I am totally broke, I thought as I sprinkled cocoa onto the foam. *And actually, he's right.*

I was looking for an empty table, when, out of the corner of my eye, I saw Julia push through the door.

"God, I am so glad to see you." I grabbed her arm.

"I can't stay very long. I have to get to SFU." Julia recently started a job as a research assistant for a professor at the community school.

The second we sat down, Julia grabbed my wrist and checked my watch. "Okay, I've got two minutes. Cool watch, by the way. What is that, a jester?"

"A harlequin. Robin bought it for me," I told Julia. Robin liked the idea of the harlequin, a performer in royal courts, since she and I were both performers.

"Nice." Julia picked up her coffee. "So you guys are sort of friends again?"

"Sort of." I followed her over to some empty chairs and sat down. "I mean, she keeps inviting me places. Robin can be a lot of fun."

"But . . . ?" Julia probed. "What's the catch?"

"No catch, really. I'm just trying to keep it sort of light for now," I answered. "It's funny. Robin thinks I'm so together. Meanwhile, my life is coming apart. Julia, I am completely broke."

Julia shrugged. "Join the club."

"No, I mean *really* broke." I told her about the bank, how I had pleaded with Ms. Templeton.

Julia bit her lip. "And you didn't get the loan?"

I shook my head. "When you have money, you can borrow anything you want. When you're broke, when you really need a loan, that's when no one will lend you a penny."

"It's true. Griffin and I learned that the hard way. With all the stuff he went through to try and save the bike shop . . ." Her voice trailed off for a moment, then she added, "I hate banks."

I nodded.

"So what's your next step?" Julia asked.

"My next step . . . is off a steep cliff," I muttered. I slumped forward and buried my hands in my face. "When this semester's over, I'm going to have to drop out of school. *Drop out*. Get a job."

"Leave Berkeley?" Julia seemed surprised. "But it's free. What's the big deal about sticking with it?"

"The big deal is registration fees. And paying for books. Lots of books. Plus, you know, *little* things like rent and food." I frowned. "A part-time job won't cover it. And there's no way I can be a full-time student with a full-time job."

Julia took a sip of latte, as if she needed time to absorb this new information. "It's hard for you—dropping out," she admitted. "I know that. But you can get a job, save some money, then go back. It's not the end of the world."

"Funny, because it definitely feels that way," I told her. "I feel like my heart is going to stop beating and I'm going to shrivel up and dry out and become this lifeless shell of a person."

"Whoa." Julia winced. "Is that . . . is that what you think of *me*? Because *I'm* not going to college?"

"No! I didn't mean that. It's just—" I stopped

myself. I didn't want to babble on and say the wrong thing.

"It's not the same," I told her slowly. "You *chose* not to go to college. I *want* to go. It's different."

She looked down into her mug and shrugged. "I guess." I could tell that she was still slightly ticked off.

"It's just . . . it's going to be a major adjustment for me," I went on. "I mean, since junior high, before that even, I just assumed I would go to college. I didn't consider any other possibilities. Even if I can go back to Berkeley in a year or two, this is not the way I wanted my life to go."

"I know you're having trouble with all this, but it's not horrible," Julia asserted. "College isn't everything."

I looked into her clear brown eyes and tried to believe her. I really did try.

But I could not imagine my life without college. So life, as I knew it, was over.

Chapter 10

Have you ever tried to pretend all your problems and fears and worries don't exist?

Most people can't. But that's what I do whenever I perform. Before I go onstage, I take a deep breath, shake off my problems, and try to spark the positive energy inside me.

Then . . . I just go for it.

That's pretty much the way it went Saturday night when our band played at the Lafayette Festival. It was held in a high school auditorium. It was pretty well organized. We got dressing rooms and refreshments and—best of all—money.

"Here's your share." Randy handed me a stack of bills. Randy is our lead guitarist and also our unofficial manager.

I still felt pumped with adrenaline from our performance. I couldn't stand still as we hung around backstage, watching the other bands.

"We each got fifty," Randy explained. "Not bad, huh?"

"Great," I muttered. "If we can do, like, three gigs a day, I might not have to drop out of Berkeley."

He gave me a blank stare. "Huh?"

"Never mind." I waved him off. I got along with the guys in the band, but we weren't close. We kept things on a strictly professional level, and so far it had worked for us.

I peeked around a giant amp, trying to get a look at the audience. The lighting made it hard to see beyond the first few rows of people. David was supposed to be out there somewhere. I got him a free pass for the festival, and we were going out afterward.

The last band took the stage, and I headed back to the dressing room. One of the stage managers touched my arm.

"Are you Sarah Reeves?" I nodded. "Your mother is here. I sent her back to the dressing room."

I froze in my tracks. *My mother?*

I hadn't seen her or my dad since Bailey's trial!

Well, it didn't matter. Nothing had changed.

I marched back to the dressing room, determined to get rid of her. There was no way I was going to pretend things were fine with my adoptive mother. I threw open the door—and found Robin and David inside.

"Robin?" I sighed with relief. "When the guy told me my mother was here, I thought. . . ."

I didn't finish the sentence. It might hurt Robin's feelings if I made it clear I didn't think of her when I heard the word "mother." But I didn't. And I probably never would. It was too late for that.

"Surprised?" Robin asked. "When you mentioned this gig, I couldn't resist. You were spectacular. That last number really shows off your range." She jumped up and gave me a kiss, sort of a show-biz peck on the cheek.

I looked to David for a reaction. He just met my mother. My *real* mother. What had they been talking about? What did she tell him about me?

"You ready to go?" David asked. He swung back and forth in his chair, looking kind of bored.

"I'd like to take my stage makeup off first." I walked over to the mirror. "Uh, did you two meet?" I asked.

"I introduced myself," Robin reported. "David says he's one of your classmates at Berkeley."

That's not all he is, I thought. *Why didn't he tell Robin that we're going out?*

"Uh—right." I reached for a jar of cold cream.

Robin grabbed a couple of tissues and tucked them into my collar. "Now you won't gunk up your shirt."

"Thanks." I started smearing the cold cream on my face.

"What class do you and Sarah have together?" Robin asked.

"Criminal justice," David told her.

Oh, wow. David got out a whole two-word answer, I thought. I hated how he sort of shut down around other people. It was borderline rude.

"Are you taking anything else that's interesting?" Robin met my eyes in the mirror and smiled.

"Not really," David said.

I wiped the cold cream off as fast as I could. This non-conversation was just too painful to listen to.

"So what did you think? Did you like our set?" I asked David.

"I missed the beginning," he admitted. "But I heard that song about the railroad."

"Our *last* song?" I turned to him. "You missed our whole act?"

"Parking is impossible in this neighborhood," he told me. "But I caught the railroad song."

I turned away from him. How could he be so rude and not even be aware of it?

"It was very moving," Robin jumped in. "That last song, and the other ballad too. The lead guitarist follows you well, and that drummer really knows how to play under a vocalist. Who chooses your material?" She shook her head. "Listen to me ramble on. I'm sorry, but I have a million questions."

"That's okay. I tend to ramble a little myself." I smiled. "And now that our performance is finished, I've got plenty of time."

"Actually, you don't." David pointed to his watch. "I'm parked on a meter. We really have to run."

I wiped a tissue across my cheek and gave him a look. I didn't want to run. I wanted to hang out with Robin, and I assumed he would too.

Then again, I assumed that he would get here in time to see my set. I was wrong.

"Why don't you just go?" I snapped.

He stood up and shot an anxious look toward the door. "Are you mad?"

"It's going to take me a while longer, and I don't want you to get a ticket." *God forbid,* I thought.

He strode toward the door. "Okay. I'll call you. Or I'll see you in class."

"Whatever," I remarked. The door closed behind him.

Robin folded her arms. "Trouble in paradise?"

"David is . . . difficult to figure out. He kind of goes hot and cold. One of my gazillion problems."

"Really?" Robin's eyes grew thoughtful. "Well, I never was very good with math, but a gazillion sounds like a lot." She swung her chair around toward me. "Why don't you sit down and give me the list . . . starting with number one."

Yeah, why didn't I? I needed someone to talk to, and Robin *wanted* to listen. I had to let her into my life at least a little, otherwise what was the point of even getting together?

I sat down and sighed. "These past few weeks, I know you thought I was, like, this perfect person. You kept going on and on about how well I've got it together. But it's just not true. I hate to tell you this— but your daughter is a mess."

Robin didn't answer. She just took a brush from my makeup kit and held it over my head. "I'll brush. You sit back and spill."

I leaned back in the chair, feeling a little better as Robin started brushing out my hair. No one had done that for me since I was a little girl.

I was getting used to being totally responsible for taking care of myself. But I have to admit it was sort of nice to be taken care of right then.

"Okay, here goes. I'm in debt. My credit cards are maxed out. I couldn't even register for next semester because I'm too broke," I told her. I rushed on, not waiting for Robin to reply. "There's late registration, but that's not going to help, because there is no way I can make my rent and my expenses and pay for school without a full-time job. And if I have a full-time job, I can't take a full course load. I'm going to have to drop out."

"Oh, Sarah, you took on a huge task all by yourself." Robin gently pulled the brush through my hair. "Most kids can't make it through college without some outside help."

"I definitely can't. I'm sunk." I wadded a tissue into a ball and tossed it onto the vanity. "I've totally botched my life." I hung my head in my hands.

Robin stopped brushing. "You have a flair for the dramatic." She smiled. "Reminds me of someone I know."

I looked up. "You?"

She nodded. "I wish you had said something to me before. I didn't even think to ask. Anyway, I'm glad that you did finally tell me. I feel good about that. And . . . I want to help."

Robin swiveled my chair around so that we were face-to-face. "Let *me* help you out with some money. I can cover your living expenses—at least until you finish school. That way, I know you'll make it through college."

I felt my jaw go slack. It was so unexpected. A—a staggering offer.

I shook my head. "But you're just an actress. How can you afford to support yourself . . . and me?"

"I'm getting money from Jeremy's estate. The funds will be released in a few weeks. He wasn't super wealthy, but there's enough for something like this. He would want this. *I* want this, Sarah. Please, let me help."

"I . . . I don't know what to say," I stammered. It was so generous, so unexpected, so—irresistible. To stay in school, it was like a chance to keep breathing. A chance to stay alive.

But taking money from Robin—that was like saying there was this *bond* between us. It was letting her into my life in a big way.

But she's not asking for anything in exchange, I thought. There are no conditions—the way there were with Mom and Dad. They wanted to pay for school only if I agreed never to see Bailey again.

Robin doesn't want anything from me. There was no "I'll give you this money *if*" with her.

I thought about our expeditions around the city. Robin was fun to hang out with. And it did seem like she planned on sticking around this time.

Then I thought how good it felt when Robin was brushing my hair. How it was kind of nice to be taken care of a little.

"Say yes," Robin urged me.

I met her gaze for a long while. Was she someone I wanted to let into my life?

"Yes," I whispered.

I felt this spontaneous urge, and I couldn't ignore it. I reached out—and hugged my mother.

Chapter 11

"Give a girl a watch and she still can't be on time," Robin called as I jogged toward her.

"I am *so* sorry." I shielded my eyes from the bright sun shining on Berkeley's campus. "The professor kept us late—so he could spring an assignment on us. One that's going to take a ton of research."

Usually I'd complain a lot more about a last-minute assignment, but I was so happy to be able to stay in school, I would have done *fifty* last-minute assignments.

"Too bad." Robin walked with me through Sather Gate. We cut across the campus plaza.

"Yeah. I was supposed to have the afternoon free. I promised I'd make David dinner tonight, and I haven't gone grocery shopping. The apartment is a disaster area. I don't know how I'm going to get everything done."

"Here's what we'll do. We'll skip the movie. It's obvious you don't have a minute to spare." She spun me around and pointed me toward the library. "You go do your research. I will go to the market for food and flowers and wine. Wait—you're not twenty-one yet—make that sparkling cider."

"This is so great of you," I told her.

"No time for talk. Let's synchronize our watches. We will meet at your apartment in exactly two hours. At that time, I will commence Operation Prepare for Date, and help you cook, shove things into closets, and sweep dust under the rugs."

I laughed. "You noticed my thorough house-keeping?"

"Like mother, like daughter." She grinned.

I smiled back. I was getting used to hearing her use the word "daughter."

Robin gave me a gentle push. "Go. Research. I'll see you at five."

I headed off, laughing to myself. Robin was a godsend. And not just because of the money. She had a way of turning a crisis inside out, transforming it into something fun. It was the way that I tried to approach problems too.

Like mother, like daughter.

"Tablecloth or place mats?" I asked Robin, who stood at the counter chopping onions.

"Hmm. The tablecloth is made of—?" she asked.

"Plastic."

"The quilted place mats. Definitely."

"That's what I thought." I slid the mats onto the

table. "They'll look nice with the candles and tulips that you bought. They smell so fresh. Where did you get them?"

"Humbold's Market. There's something so great about fresh flowers. We always had them at home. My parents owned a flower shop." She put down the knife and motioned me over. "Now, I want you to watch and learn, because this is the easiest, cheapest, most delicious meal you will ever make in your life.

"Always use fresh tomatoes," she explained as she combined the ingredients for her special rice and bean casserole. "And cut down on the butter by using chicken stock."

"Where did you get this recipe?" I asked.

"I'm an actress." She laughed. "It was inspired by poverty. And I wanted something I could serve my agent."

Side by side, we cooked and dusted and vacuumed. Before long the apartment was under control, suddenly a pleasant, inviting place to be. I began to relax a little. Thanks to Robin, things were going smoothly. But the night still loomed before me.

There was David, so hard to read. And David's expectations, and . . . the things that I wanted. But was I ready?

"Looks like everything is under control here," Robin observed. She wiped her hands on a dishtowel. "Though *you* still look a little stressed."

I shrugged. I mean, Robin *was* my mother. How technical do you get when you're telling your mother about your sex life? Or lack thereof.

"Maybe I should go and give you a chance to unwind a little," she offered.

"No, that's not it. It's David . . . and me." I looked up at her and laughed. "This is weird. Awkward, I mean. But I'm sort of a wreck. He's been pressuring me to . . . well, it's about having . . . you know, sex."

She didn't seem to be surprised or embarrassed. Not at all. "Hmm. That's a key issue in a relationship."

"Well, at the moment, it's the *only* issue for David and me," I answered. "And it just won't go away. I mean, I don't know if I want it to go away. I don't know what I want. When I'm with him, I'm definitely attracted to him. But there's something holding me back. I'm just not sure. I don't know if I'm ready."

I figured I should tell her *everything*. "It's all kind of complicated by the fact that I've never . . . So it's one of those major life decisions."

Robin took my hands. "This is going to sound incredibly old-fashioned, Sarah, but be true to yourself. Wait until you are completely ready. If he loves you, he won't mind."

I looked down at her hands—hands that were so much like mine, same long fingers, same slim wrists. The master mold.

"I guess you see yourself in me," I said. "You know . . . having sex. Getting pregnant. And you're afraid that I'll make the same mistake you made."

Robin's eyes misted over with tears as she squeezed my hands. "No, Sarah, no," she whispered. "Having you was not a mistake. I mean, I can see that so clearly now."

I was shocked . . . and a little surprised. For some reason, I wanted to cry too. It was . . . the most tender moment we had ever shared.

She shook her head, adding, "Having you was the best thing . . . the most worthwhile thing I have ever done in my life."

Chapter **12**

Bing! The timer on the stove rang. Robin pulled open the oven to check on the quick bread she was making to go with the casserole.

We both swiped at our eyes and let the subject drop—but I would never forget that moment. Never.

With everything under control, Robin headed off and I jumped into the shower. The pressure that had been weighing me down all day seemed lighter somehow, and as I dried my hair I thought about Robin's advice.

I had to do what was best for *me*—if I could figure out what that was.

Then suddenly I just knew. The answer seemed so obvious. Why had I been torturing myself over this?

By the time the doorbell rang, I felt really good about my decision. I went to the door. David stood in the hall with a bouquet of carnations in one hand and a wrapped box tucked under the other arm.

"Whoa. David, hi!" I exclaimed. "What's all this? It's not my birthday or anything."

"It's a special day." He handed me the flowers. "At least, we can make it special."

"Uh—sure," I motioned him inside. While I found a vase for the flowers, I told him about my hectic afternoon. "Robin really saved the day."

"Really?" David slipped off his leather jacket and tossed it onto a chair. "Does she always push her way into the middle of things? We didn't get to go out after your concert because *she* wouldn't take a hint and leave."

"Hey, you wouldn't have anything to eat tonight if it weren't for her. She really helped me out," I defended Robin.

I felt like pointing out that David didn't have to take off after the concert. He and Robin and I could have hung out together for a while. Later the two of us would totally have gotten our chance to be alone.

I quickly decided not to get into it. I mean, it's not like he was the only guy who wasn't crazy about spending time with his girlfriend's mother.

"Do you want to eat now?" I asked. I opened the stove and slipped my hands into oven mitts. "Because everything is ready."

David shrugged. "Sure, let's . . . eat." He sat down at the table as if he just wanted to get this whole dinner thing over with.

As I served the casserole and salad and sat down to eat, I watched him, sort of studying him. What was he thinking? I wished David would talk a little more.

The silence made me sort of nervous, and I started doing my babbling thing.

"So my professor gave us this last-minute assignment, which I knew I had to do today, since you and I are going to Alcatraz tomorrow for our research, and I figured that we'd need Sunday to write up our notes if we want to get the project in on time. You should have seen me bulldoze my way through the library—"

"Oh, didn't I tell you about tomorrow?" he interrupted.

"Tomorrow?" I asked. "No, I don't . . . what?"

"I have to work," he said. "So I figured we could split things up. You go to Alcatraz and I'll write up your notes."

"You can't go?" I put down my fork. "But I thought we were doing this project together."

"The manager put me in the schedule," he defended himself. "There's nothing I can do about it."

"Oh. Okay, I guess." I took a bite of Robin's bread. "What do you think of the casserole?"

"It's pretty good," he answered.

He was totally oblivious of the fact that I'd cleaned up and lit candles and gone all-out to make things nice for him. And he was backing out of our project—something we'd planned for weeks—and acting as if it were no big deal.

Suddenly I lost my appetite. Without a word I swung my feet to the floor and carried my plate to the sink.

He followed me into the kitchen. "You're mad," he stated.

I didn't answer.

"Look, I'm sorry about tomorrow. They sprung it

on me at the last minute," he explained. "You know I want to go with you."

"Do you?" I stared down into the sink. "Do you *really,* David? Because you are *so* hard to read, and when I do get signals from you, they are totally mixed up."

"I'm sorry." He turned me away from the sink and pulled me into his arms. "Okay, here's a new signal. Let's see if you can figure this out."

He leaned down and brushed his lips over mine gently, sort of teasing.

He wasn't perfect. But he *was* a good kisser. "Mmm." I smiled up at him. "You're trying to say that you like my lip gloss?"

"Wrong." He leaned down and kissed me again.

This time I sighed, relaxing in his arms.

"That's right," he whispered. "I think you're getting it."

I closed my eyes as his hands swept through my hair. I was getting this shivering sensation that increased as his hands moved down my back.

My pulse hammered in my ears as I leaned into his chest, lost in sensation. This was something that we could do together. This was the place where David and I were in synch.

He was right about one thing. When it came to physical attraction, we communicated well.

But it wasn't enough. Feeling good was one thing. But sex with David would be just that—physical attraction without any real bond beneath the surface.

I took a deep breath and pushed away from his chest.

"I'm sorry," I whispered. "But I can't. It's . . . it's just not right for me now."

He froze for a moment, a muscle working in his jaw as he studied me. Then he smiled. "That's right, you told me about your fantasy. The perfect elements for the perfect night."

He went into the living room and picked up the wrapped package. "Well, we've got plenty of flowers. The music is right. And I brought you this—" He handed the package to me. "Go ahead. Open it."

I shook my head. "David—"

"Go on," he insisted.

I tore off the gold foil paper and opened the box. Inside were ivory sheets edged in lacy eyelet. They were precisely the sheets I had envisioned in my fantasy.

But they were all wrong.

"David, this is not about flowers and sheets." I really wanted to make him understand.

But he didn't want to hear me. "Come on, Sarah. I'll help you put them on the bed."

"No, David . . . no." I blocked his path to the bedroom. "The truth is, I'm just not ready. *We're* not ready. There's still so much that we don't know about each other."

He raised his eyebrows. "My favorite color is blue. I was born in Seattle. And my middle name is Paul."

"It's not a joke," I declared. "It's hard for me too. But just because there's this physical thing between us, it doesn't mean we have a relationship. I don't know that much about you or your friends . . . and there are so many things you don't know about me."

"Oh, come on," he snapped. "Do I have to take an exam in the history of Sarah?"

"You would fail. Because you don't know that much about me. Not really," I answered.

"Look, I know that I *love* you, and I *want* you. And that's enough for me." Anger flashed in his dark eyes. "Would you just stop thinking so much and let things happen?"

My jaw dropped. I stared up at him. Had he really said the word *love?* It was the first time he'd ever used the word. And in such a nasty tone. It floored me. Did he really think I'd have sex with him if he pressured me enough?

I shook my head. "You'd better go."

He stepped back, as if he couldn't believe that I would turn him away. "If I leave now, this is over. I'm not coming back, Sarah."

He was pushing again, and I was getting sick of it. I marched to the door and pulled it open.

"You know what?" I gritted my teeth. "That's probably best for both of us."

He stormed out the door without looking back. I hurled the box of sheets after him. "You can take these with you!" I yelled, and slammed the door.

How could he say that he loved me? The guy didn't know the meaning of the word. He didn't have a clue.

I strode into the kitchen, grabbed his plate off the table, and dumped it into the sink. I turned on the water full force and washed away all traces of David.

I picked up the casserole dish. There was still enough left for another meal—thanks to Robin.

Robin . . .

She had come through for me today. Pitching in when someone needed help. Listening to their problems, maybe giving a little good advice. That was what love was all about. Maybe someday David would wake up and figure that out.

I covered the dish with foil and slid it into the fridge, then I collapsed on the sofa.

What had really happened tonight? I had lost a boyfriend who didn't really care about me. No biggie.

Because I had found a mother who loved me.

And that was pretty amazing.

Chapter 13

So I tossed him out, along with his box of sheets," I told Robin. It was Saturday morning, and we were talking on the phone, going over the "highlights" of my date with David.

Robin laughed. "Good. I hope he had trouble getting his money back from the store."

"Oh, he'll probably just save them for the next girlfriend," I told her. "Slime mold."

"I'm glad that you're not crying in your cereal."

"Nope. No loss," I answered. "Except that I've got to go to Alcatraz alone. It's this project for my criminal justice class. So I was wondering, if you're not doing anything today. . . ."

It was the first time I'd taken the initiative and invited Robin to do something with me.

"Alcatraz? We could do that," Robin told me. "If I

can drag myself out of these sweats and throw together some breakfast."

"Hey, it's my turn to be the organizer," I told her. "You get ready, and I'll meet you at your apartment with coffee and croissants."

"Sounds like a plan," Robin said.

"I'm halfway there," Robin called when I arrived. She was dressed in jeans and a fisherman's sweater. Her hair was wrapped in a thick towel.

"Take your time." I slid my bags onto the kitchen table. I pulled out a paper cup and handed it to Robin. "This is yours. And I got half a dozen croissants."

"Jeez, Sarah. That should last me until the new millennium."

"Are you kidding? I'll polish them off before your hair is dry," I teased.

Robin toasted me with her coffee cup. "Save *one* for me. This won't take long." She headed into the bedroom, and a moment later I heard the whining sound of a blow dryer.

I sat down at the kitchen table and dug into a buttery roll. I picked up a magazine from the huge stack on the chair next to me. From the looks of things, Robin did a lot of reading. I was checking out the new spring fashions when the phone rang.

"Robin?" I called.

The blow dryer continued to whir. I decided to let the machine get it.

I only half listened when Robin's recording went on.

"Leave a message after the tone. . . ." *Beep.*

"Robin, it's Dr. Kaufman." The male voice

sounded solid and steady. "From San Francisco General."

What? I looked up from the magazine.

"My office has been trying to reach you. I hate to leave this on your machine. Would you call me? Robin, your latest test results are in, and we're approaching a critical stage."

Critical stage? A horrible feeling seeped through me. Robin was—*sick?*

I leapt up and hurried over to the machine. It's like I thought I'd hear more if I got closer.

"Time is of the essence," the doctor went on. "Let's get that daughter of yours in to see if she's a suitable match. Okay? Call me. Bye."

The light on the machine began to blink as the line clicked off. And all I could do was stare. Robin was sick. And the doctor mentioned something about her daughter. *Me.* What did it mean?

I was still staring at the machine when Robin popped her head into the kitchen.

"Is it cold? Should I do a layer thing, or do you think . . ." Her voice trailed off as we locked eyes. "Sarah, you're scaring me. What's wrong."

I pointed at the machine. "There's a message. The hospital called . . . Dr. something, I don't know." My chest felt tight, as if a heavy weight were crushing down on me. "He said you were approaching a critical phase. He said something about . . . about testing your daughter."

Robin covered her mouth. All the color drained out of her face. "I didn't . . . you weren't supposed to hear about it. At least, not that way."

I shook my head. The weight in my chest was

getting worse; it was a struggle to breathe. "So how was I—how was I supposed to hear about it? Tell me now . . . the truth. What's going on?"

Robin folded her arms across her chest and stared at the floor. "The truth is that I *am* sick." She looked up, and from the pinched look around her eyes I could see that she was afraid.

I wondered if I looked the same way. Because I was scared too. Really scared. "How bad . . . What . . ." I couldn't even form a complete sentence.

"I need a bone marrow transplant, Sarah. It's almost impossible to find a donor. It usually has to be a blood relative. And . . ."

A bone marrow transplant. That meant cancer, didn't it? I wrapped my arms around myself. Suddenly I felt cold.

"Wait. *A blood relative?*" The second part of what Robin said hit me. "Is that why your doctor mentioned me?"

"Maybe you should sit down," Robin suggested.

"I don't want to sit down." I couldn't stop staring at her. She looked like a stranger. Did I even know this person?

"I'm your only living relative." I struggled to keep my voice from shaking. "That means *I'm* your only chance of a match."

Robin sighed. "God, I am so sorry you had to hear about it this way."

"No," I insisted. "No, this is good. Because I hate it—I absolutely *hate* it—when people hide the truth from me. And that's what you've been doing, right? I mean, it's all been an act—the whole *mother* thing."

"Sarah, no—" Robin stepped forward and reached her hand out for me.

DON'T SAY YOU LOVE ME

I backed away from her. "The gifts. The advice. The stories about stuff that happened when you grew up. It was all to get me to care about you—so you could get what you wanted from me."

"No. No, Sarah." Robin's throat worked as she struggled not to cry.

"I forgot that you were an *actress*," I said. "You're very good at it, you know. *Acting,* I mean."

"It wasn't an act," Robin insisted, her voice husky.

"Sure. I'm supposed to believe that now. Why not? I'm such a sucker for a snow job. Good old Sarah, she's so gullible." I reached for my jacket and bag. "How could I be such a moron?"

"You're not." Robin put her hand on my arm, trying to stop me from leaving.

"Don't touch me," I cried, breaking free. "Haven't you done enough to screw up my life? God, you abandoned me *twice.* Then you come back and hurt me all over again!"

Robin didn't have an answer for that. She just kind of collapsed onto a kitchen chair.

"Don't call me or write me or drive down my block," I told her. "I don't want to see you—ever again."

Chapter 14

My eyes were flooded with tears. I could hardly see the road. But I couldn't stop driving. I had to get away from Robin—far away.

I swiped my hands across my cheeks and pressed on the gas pedal. *Think of something else,* I ordered myself. *Think of skiing. And performing. And French lit. And Sno-Kones. And the Salingers' big Victorian house.*

Yes! I had to see Julia, and I had to do it now. There was no way I'd make it through this day alone.

When I reached a red light, I took a deep breath and put on my turn signal. The light changed and I turned right, toward the Salingers'. I thought a little noise and chaos would be just the thing to make me feel better.

I was wrong.

"You look awful," Julia observed. I crossed the

kitchen, tripping over a plastic barn and scattering the animals.

"Hey!" Owen stamped his foot at me. "Don't wreck it!"

"Calm down, Owen. She didn't mean it," Julia scolded him.

"It's not his fault," Claudia defended their youngest brother. "He spent the last half hour setting all those animals up in little lines and everything."

"I'm sorry, Owen." I covered my face with my hands.

"Hey, Sarah." Charlie brushed past me on the way to the fridge. "You okay?"

"I'm fine," I insisted.

"Because you look a little pale," Charlie went on. He pulled a bottle off the top shelf. "Do you want some carrot juice? It's loaded with beta-carotene and—"

"No," I snapped. The sight of the thick orange liquid made my stomach turn over.

"Can someone drive me to the library?" Claudia asked.

"Julia, I really need to—" I began.

"Can't you take the bus?" Julia asked her sister.

Owen thrust a plastic cow into my hand. "Fix it!" he demanded. He held up one of the cow's legs. I guess I snapped it off when I stepped on it.

"I don't know how," I told him.

"Fix it!" he yelled.

"I just—I—oh, never mind." I turned away and headed out the door. For some reason, the same chaos that I usually found reassuring was driving me completely over the edge today.

I was halfway across the yard, when I heard the door open behind me.

"Sarah? Wait!" It was Julia. She ran over and fell into step beside me.

"Did I forget something?" I asked.

"Yeah." She slipped on her leather jacket and flipped her dark hair over the collar. "You forgot that we've been friends for, like, eons. And I can read you like a book. I may be wrapped up in other things, but I'd have to be blind not to see that you're upset. What's up?"

I sighed. "Do you have an hour or two?"

"For you? The whole day," Julia answered.

"Are you up for a trip to Alcatraz?" I asked.

Less than an hour later, we were on a ferry over to tour the island. Is Julia a great friend, or what?

"Escape *to* Alcatraz," Julia joked. She popped on her sunglasses. "This isn't such a bad thing to do for homework."

I tried to smile, but I know it came out more like a grimace. I slumped down on the nearest bench. Julia sat down next to me.

"Okay, start talking," Julia ordered. "I was going to try and wait until you were ready, but I can't take the suspense."

I didn't feel ready to go into the whole Robin thing, so I started with one of my smaller problems. "I broke up with David," I blurted out.

"Oh. I'm sorry," Julia said. "Or *should* I be sorry?"

"You don't have to be that sorry," I answered. "He turned out to be sort of a jerk. He kept saying how he wanted our time together to be a vacation. Which seemed kind of romantic at first." I took a deep breath of the salty air. "But it really meant he wanted to know only the happy, perky, *optimistic* Sarah. He didn't want to hear about any problems or anything. He just wanted to have fun."

"Translation—have sex," Julia guessed.

"You got it," I answered.

"So, did you?" The wind kept blowing Julia's hair into her face.

"No, thank God," I answered. The ferry gave a lurch as it docked. I grabbed my bag. We headed down the boat ramp, then hiked up the steep hill to the old prison.

"Is there anything you want me to do? You know, to help with your paper?" Julia asked as we started inside.

"No, I just really wanted company," I admitted. We walked down a wide corridor surrounded by bars and cinder blocks. Despite the beauty of the island, the prison was not a pretty place. Stuffy, cold, and cramped—not the sort of place you'd call home. I jotted down a few notes, then followed Julia into a tiny cell—a typical living space for a prisoner.

"A little cramped," Julia joked. "But, hey, they cook all your meals. And these days I think most prisons even get cable TV."

"Maybe I should move in," I said. "It sounds like an improvement over my life."

"Really?" I could hear the concern in Julia's voice. "Sarah, you seem so unhappy. But when you talked about David, you sounded kind of over it. There's more going on, isn't there?"

I nodded, staring through the bars.

"Are you going to tell me? Or do I have to find one of the old interrogation rooms and turn on a white light or something?"

I had to tell Julia. That's why I brought her out here.

"It's not just David. It's Robin," I admitted.

"Your mother?"

"I was at her apartment this morning. . . ." I gulped. Suddenly this huge lump had formed in my throat. "She got this message on her answering machine from a doctor. He said . . . he said that she had to get her daughter in to see him soon—because she had reached a . . . a critical stage."

Julia handed me a tissue and I realized tears were spilling down my cheeks. "Robin needs a bone marrow transplant—and I'm the most likely match, I deduced."

I scrubbed my face with the tissue. "She used me. Completely. A couple of lunches and I was convinced she really cared about me."

Julia wrapped her arm around my shoulders. "Don't blame yourself. She's your mother. Ever since you found out you were adopted, you've wanted a relationship with her."

"But she did it to me before, remember?" I demanded. "She acted like she wanted to know me, to be in my life, and then she took off. She didn't even give me her new address. I'm such a complete idiot!"

"No. *She's* the idiot. She could have this wonderful daughter in her life, and she blew it," Julia insisted. "Sounds pretty dumb to me."

"If I'm so wonderful, why does she keep leaving?" I mumbled.

"Don't even think that." Julia pulled me around to face her. "Don't let her make you start feeling bad about yourself. You're this amazing, beautiful, smart person. Everyone who knows you loves you."

Not everyone, I thought. *Not everyone.*

Chapter 15

I pulled on my robe and padded into the kitchen in my bare feet. Three A.M., and I couldn't fall asleep. Big surprise.

I pulled open the refrigerator door. The light inside gleamed on the nearly bare shelves. I had a choice of leftover casserole, apples, eggs, and milk.

"I guess it's hot chocolate," I said to myself.

"Make that two." Bailey stood in the doorway, wearing sweat pants and a T-shirt.

"What are you doing up?" I asked him.

He rubbed his eyes. "You started it."

"I can't sleep." I pulled out a pot and measured two mugs of milk into it. "I may never sleep again."

"Robin?" he questioned.

"What else?" I told Bailey the whole story earlier

that night. And he was totally there for me. Listening. Understanding.

"So, what are you going to do—about the transplant?" he asked.

I turned down the burner. I stirred the milk so hard, it splashed onto the stove, sizzling. "Why should I do it? Why should I do anything for her? She lied to me. She manipulated me. Maybe if she'd been honest from the beginning. . . ."

"It would have been sort of hard to knock on the door and say 'Hi. Long time no see. Can I have some bone marrow?'" Bailey argued.

I stared at him. "Are you saying what she did was right?"

"No," Bailey defended himself. "It was totally and completely wrong. There's no excuse for it. But, God, Sarah, what if she dies. What if she dies, and you could have—"

"That's not my problem," I interrupted. I pulled two mugs out of the cupboard and slammed them onto the counter.

Bailey sat down at the kitchen table. He didn't say anything else. He just watched me.

I grabbed the saucepan and dumped the milk into the first mug. Steaming droplets spattered across my hand. I dropped the pan and stuck my hand under the cold water.

My shoulders shook as sobs tore through my body.

Bailey came up behind me and slid his hands around my waist. "Hey, are you okay?"

"Oh, Bay. Why do I *care?*" I choked out. "After everything she did, why do I still *care?*"

"Because you're Sarah," Bailey stated. He reached around me and turned off the water. Then he gently dried my hand. "That doesn't look too bad."

"I've got to go for the test, don't I?" I said.

Bailey nodded. "I think you do. And don't worry. I'll help you deal with Robin. You don't even have to talk to her if you don't want to."

"Thanks, Bay." I slipped my hands around his huge frame and gave him a hug.

At least I still had my friends.

"I hate hospitals," Julia muttered under her breath. "Ever since Charlie got sick. The smell, the corridors, the paperwork . . . it's really awful."

"Thanks for coming with me," I told her.

"Of course. There was no way I was going to let you do this alone," Julia answered.

Julia and Bailey had really come through for me. Bailey spent all morning on the phone, tracking down Robin's doctor, arranging things. Then Julia picked me up and drove me over here.

I picked up an ancient magazine from the table near the nurses' station.

"The worst part about tests is usually the waiting," Julia commented.

I nodded. When Bailey and I crashed in his Jeep, I'd been in the hospital overnight, mostly for observation. It was no big deal. I mean, for me the worst part of the whole thing had been worrying about Bailey. Back then he was totally messed up, drinking too much. We're all lucky that he got some help and turned his life around.

"Ms. Reeves?" a nurse called.

"I'll be right here, waiting for you," Julia whispered as I stood up.

The nurse led me into a small room set up with the usual medical stuff—gauze and sterile tools and swabs.

"Try to relax," she instructed. "I can't say that this is painless. I wish we could screen with a simple blood test, but in this case we need to do a medical procedure that usually takes from one to three hours."

I leaned against the table and nodded. Just my luck. It couldn't be quick and simple. I'd have to spend half the day here.

The nurse handed me a blue hospital gown. "We'll use a local anesthesia, but afterward you may experience some cramping. Now, let me find the doctor while you get changed."

I changed quickly, trying to block Robin out of my mind.

Pretend it's a routine test, I told myself. *Pretend you're giving blood. Don't think about what might happen if you are a match and Robin needs you. Or if you are not a match and Robin . . .*

No. I wouldn't even allow myself to think about that.

I heard a light knock on the door, and the nurse returned with a heavyset man with a trim beard and warm eyes.

"Dr. Shendy, a hematologist, will be doing the procedure," the nurse reported.

"Hello, Sarah." He shook my hand. "Why don't you sit up on the table and we'll get started?"

"Great," I mumbled. "The sooner I get this over with, the better."

"It's good of you to come in," the doctor added.

"Yeah," I muttered.

Each step of the procedure Dr. Shendy told me what to expect before he went ahead. And the nurse kept assuring me that everything was fine. It wasn't that painful or anything, but I was glad when it was over.

"Dr. Kaufman—he's your mother's doctor—will get back to you with the results," the nurse told me when they had given me the okay to leave. "If you don't hear, you can call us directly. We should know in two to three days."

"Thanks," I said. When she left, I changed back into my street clothes as quickly as I could. I wanted out of there. I headed into the waiting room. It felt good to see Julia right where I left her. There were still *some* people I could count on.

"All done," I told her.

"Sarah?" a voice called from behind me.

I didn't want to turn around. Because I knew it was Robin, and I didn't want to see her. Ever. I had learned my lesson. I wasn't going to let Robin into my life again.

"Sarah!" she repeated.

I slowly turned to face her.

She rushed toward me. "I didn't know you . . . I was here for tests and I saw your name on the sign-in sheet and . . . well, the nurse explained. I wanted to thank you."

You got your specimen! I wanted to shout. *I thought you wanted a daughter, but you have just what you really wanted—a lab rat!*

But if I said that, Robin would go into her *act*. I would have to watch her pretend to care about me. I just couldn't take that.

Julia hurried over to me. I grabbed my jacket from her, squeezed past Robin, and walked out of there without a word.

Chapter 16

I had to call. I mean, it had been two days with no word from Dr. Kaufman. How long was I supposed to wait?

I picked up the phone, punched in a few numbers, then hung up and wiped my sweaty palms on my jeans. It was stupid to call. If they had results, they would be in touch, right?

But maybe they had lost my number . . .

I picked up the phone again just as Bailey came in the door.

"Hey, what's up?" he asked.

"Nothing," I said, putting down the phone. I stared at it, hoping it would ring. But I couldn't stand just waiting, so I grabbed it up again.

"What's got you so wired?" Bailey asked. "Are you going to make a call, or are you just training for the Olympic phone team?"

I held out the phone to him. "Will you do it for me?" I pleaded. "I'm dying to know, but I can't make the call."

"The call?" Bailey looked puzzled.

"To the hospital. For the test results. I know it's crazy, but even though I want to know I . . . I sort of don't."

Bailey nodded as my explanation sank in. "No problem." He took the phone. "I don't mind making the call." He took the card I handed him and punched in the number. "Actually, I think I'm good at this stuff. I could be an agent or a personal manager or something."

I sank onto the couch and huddled there, my arms wrapped around my knees. The tension was killing me; I had to know the answer.

"Yes, I'm calling for the results of a bone marrow sample that was taken a few days ago," Bailey said. "The patient's name is Sarah Reeves." He listened for a moment, then frowned. "No, of course not. But she . . . okay, hold on."

He held the phone against his chest. "They can't give me the results. Something about confidentiality."

I sprang up and grabbed the phone from him. "This is Sarah Reeves," I said breathlessly.

"Okay, Sarah," the woman said. "We'll need your social security number for verification." I rattled off the numbers and squeezed my eyes shut as I waited.

Let me be a match. The thought just sprang into my mind. *Let me be a match so Robin won't die.*

"Let's see. You should be hearing from Dr. Kaufman, but according to this analysis, the results are negative," she told me. "That means you are not a viable bone marrow donor for Robin Merrill."

"Oh."

It was over. I could walk away knowing I had done everything I could. If, if *something* happened to Robin, well, it wouldn't be my fault.

I looked over at Bailey, who held out his hands as if to say: *What's the story?* I shook my head.

"Thanks," I said to the nurse. "Thanks a lot." I hung up, feeling strange. Not happy, not sad. Just sort of empty. Hollowed out.

"So you weren't a match?" Bailey asked quietly.

"Nope. I'm off the hook."

"Yeah, I guess so. Look, I'm sorry. About Robin," Bailey said, his blue eyes searching mine.

"Don't be. I'm relieved," I insisted. At that moment I just wanted Bailey to go away. I didn't want to talk about this. I didn't want to think about it. It was over, right? At least my part was over. I just wanted to let it be over.

"I've done everything that I can do. Now I don't have to feel guilty about cutting Robin out of my life," I told him.

"Really?" Bailey didn't seem to be convinced. "Because I'm not sure that it's going to be that easy. I mean, she *is* your mother. And she's really sick."

"It's over," I said firmly.

But I wasn't sure who I was trying to convince—Bailey or me.

"Okay, how does this sound?" Julia asked, spreading a section of the newspaper out on the carpet. "Multibillion-dollar corporation is seeking a highly motivated individual for outstanding customer service opportunity—"

"Sounds great!" I leaned over her shoulder to check

out the ad. "Except that it's in Seattle." I sat back and sighed. "Sort of a long commute."

The help wanted section of the newspaper covered the living room floor of my apartment. Julia and I were looking for jobs. Julia was hoping she could find something that paid a little better than working for the professor, and I was looking for a part-time job that would pay me enough to go to school full-time.

As if, right? But Julia insisted that it couldn't hurt to look.

"Okay, that covers the C's," Julia said, turning the page. "Onto the next category—data entry clerks."

"Didn't you try that?" I asked.

She frowned. "Yeah, and it's awful. That brings us up to dental. Dental tech, dental assistant . . . but these jobs require experience."

"I've had teeth since I was two," I said. "That's like, seventeen years of experience."

Julia smiled. "Do you want the dental listings?"

I stood up and went into the kitchen to get a drink. "Keep moving. Who wants to spend all day staring into people's mouths anyway."

Bailey opened the door and tramped in. "Here's the mail," he said, handing me a stack of letters.

"It's soggy," I said, shaking off a few drops.

"Yeah, it's raining like crazy." Bailey slipped off his wet letter jacket and gestured toward the scattered help wanted section. "Any luck?"

"Not unless we go to dental school," Julia muttered.

I flipped past the electric bill and a postcard from a department store having a sale. I came to a plain white envelope addressed to me. There was no return address on it anywhere.

"Strange," I muttered. I tore it open and out spilled a pale yellow slip of paper. A check. A check for thousands of dollars.

My heart raced for a moment. Then I read the signature—Robin Merrill. "Oh, my gosh. She did it."

"What?" Bailey glanced over my shoulder and whistled. "Whoa. That's fantastic!"

When Julia shot me a curious look, I explained. "It's a check from Robin. A really generous check from Robin. I didn't think after everything that happened . . ."

"So," Julia said, folding up a section of the paper. "Your job search is over. That must be a relief."

I shook my head. "I wish I could keep it. It would make things so easy."

"But . . . what?" Bailey prodded. "Of course you're going to take it. This check is the difference between four years of college followed by some great job or dropping out of Berkeley and being a french fry girl to make ends meet. You've got to keep it."

"Look, I want Robin out of my life," I told them. "If I take the money, she's in, big-time."

"Are you sure you want to give it back?" Julia asked. "Because—she told you the money was yours. It was a gift, a gift you already accepted."

Her dark hair fell away from her face as she looked up at me. "I know you have principles, Sarah. And that's important. It's one of the things that makes you who you are. But I just get this—this feeling that this gift is from Robin's heart. A sincere gift. If you refuse it, you're going to hurt Robin a lot. Do you really want to do that?"

I was trying to keep from getting hurt *myself*. Was I

supposed to be worrying about Robin's feelings? I mean, I know she's sick, but she still did a really rotten thing to me.

"I don't know," I told Julia, staring at the check. My head was spinning with questions. Was it right? Should I keep it? Or should I send it back?

"I just don't know."

This is crazy, I thought as I walked up to the door of Robin's apartment.

I kept saying I wanted Robin out of my life.

But here I was, knocking on the door to her apartment.

Why? The check.

I mean, Bailey was right. That money could see me through to my senior year of Berkeley. I could be clear of debt, free to concentrate on my studies. I couldn't resist.

But I couldn't take the money without talking to Robin first. If I got the feeling that she thought the check bought her some piece of me, I was out of there. I'd already gone through that with Mom and Dad, who thought they could control me with money.

I knocked again. I didn't hear anyone moving around inside. Just my luck . . . it looked like Robin wasn't home.

I turned away. I was halfway down the hall, when another door opened. It was a neighbor, an older woman I had seen once or twice while visiting Robin.

"Oh, hello, dear." She eyed me curiously. "Would you mind walking this down to the recycle bin for me?" She gestured to a bunch of newspapers tucked under one arm.

"No problem," I said, taking the stack.

She nodded toward Robin's door. "Was that you knocking? Because she's gone."

"Gone?" I glanced back toward Robin's door. "You mean she left town?"

"No." The elderly woman pursed her lips, causing wrinkles to form around her mouth. "An ambulance came for her. She's in the hospital."

Chapter 17

I have to see Robin. I have to see Robin. I have to see Robin. The words pounded through my head as my wipers whipped back and forth across my windshield.

I took a left at the light and went up the hill, driving by rote until I turned into the parking lot of San Francisco General.

I have to see Robin.

Something had clicked inside me when that woman told me about the ambulance, and I was scared. Really scared.

Yeah, I'd thought about how sick Robin was. I'd even thought about her dying. But it never felt a hundred percent real—until now.

I jumped out of the car and rushed inside. Fortunately, I remembered my way through the maze of corridors and elevators. I ran to the desk and leaned over the counter to get the nurse's attention.

"I'm looking for Robin Merrill," I said breathlessly. "She's here, isn't she?"

"Yes, she is. And you are . . . ?" the nurse asked.

"Sarah Reeves. Her daughter."

She nodded. "Robin has been asking for you."

"She has?" My voice squeaked. "Did she . . . what did she say?"

"She's heavily sedated," the nurse said, avoiding the question. "Some medications cause patients to ramble on."

"Is she okay?" I asked. "Can I see her?"

"I don't know if that's a good idea," she answered, checking her watch. "Visiting hours are over, and she really needs to rest."

She paused for a moment, studying me. "You do know that she's in a critical phase."

I swallowed hard, trying to calculate what that might mean. Exactly how critical was critical? "Please, can I see her, just for a few minutes?"

The nurse looked down the corridor and shrugged. "I guess it would be okay. It's so quiet now. But don't wake her up."

"I won't . . . I promise."

Not sure what to expect, I sort of held my breath as I followed the nurse down the hall to a small, dimly lit room. Monitors clicked and blinked over the bed where Robin lay sleeping. She looked pale and slender under the crisp sheets, sort of like a china doll who's been put to bed in a dark dollhouse.

So fragile, I thought.

The nurse checked the monitors, then disappeared.

One of Robin's hands had fallen against the bed rail, and I picked it up and placed it on the blanket. Her fingers were cold, and I wanted to rub her hand to warm it, but I was afraid to wake her up.

I leaned close. I started to whisper something like: "Everything will be fine," but I stopped myself.

I couldn't do it. It was a lie. And I wasn't going to lie to her.

Tears burned my throat, and I backed away from the bed. I couldn't stay here like this. God, what if she woke up and saw me crying my eyes out?

Quietly, I turned and crept out of the room. The fluorescent lights of the corridor hurt my eyes. I was staring down at the tile floor when someone called my name.

I looked up to see a guy in his thirties, motioning to me from the nurses' station. Dressed in a shirt and tie, he had dark hair and dark, friendly eyes. And he was young. Like one of those actors playing a doctor on a TV soap opera. The only thing that signaled "doctor" was the stethoscope around his neck.

"Stacey told me that Robin's daughter was here," he said when I reached him. "I'm Dr. Kaufman, head of your mother's team."

"Hi." I shook his hand, feeling a little uncomfortable. He seemed nice enough, but it was weird having everyone at the hospital know I was Robin's daughter. They had to have a totally wrong idea about what my relationship with Robin had been in the past. And what it was really like now.

"I was sorry to learn about the test results," he said, glancing away. "We were pinning a lot of hope on you."

I frowned. "What about another donor?" I asked. "There's got to be someone else."

"I'm sure you've heard how rare it is to find a match outside the family. Sometimes it works out for us. Sometimes people get lucky. Your mother wasn't so fortunate."

Your mother. The words sounded so weird, so unnatural. I felt as if I were overhearing someone else's conversation.

His dark eyes grew serious. "I wish there were other family members to screen, but you're Robin's only living relative. In a case like this . . . I'm afraid we're running out of options."

"So what can you do? What are you doing now?" I asked.

"We're still trying drug therapy," he said, pushing his dark hair away from his forehead. "But we're not getting the results we'd hoped for."

I shook my head, trying to see through the tears that were forming in my eyes. This whole scene was totally surreal. I felt like I was in a really bad soap opera. One of those really manipulative tear-jerkers.

This guy was too young to be a doctor. I didn't feel like anyone's daughter. This corridor was too cold and hollow and brightly lit to be real.

"I can't believe I'm hearing this," I said, swallowing a sob. "Isn't there something you can do?"

"To be honest, I'm not optimistic about Robin's chances," he said quietly. "She might make it through this crisis. Maybe a few more months. But after that—" He took a deep breath.

"Go on. Say it. She's going to die." I needed to hear the truth.

He dropped a hand onto my shoulder and nodded. "Without a transplant, we're going to lose her."

Chapter 18

Your mother . . .
We're going to lose her.
Robin's daughter.

The words rang in my ears as I drove home from the hospital.

I wanted to explain to the nurse that I wasn't really Robin's daughter. I wanted to shout at Dr. Kaufman that this was totally unfair. That I shouldn't have to stand there, crying over the awful update on Robin's condition.

"You see, the thing is, she's really not my mother," I wanted to tell them all. *"Robin gave me away when I was four days old. So the mother-daughter thing doesn't really apply here. It doesn't count."*

I pulled into a parking spot outside the apartment and burst into tears all over again. Because none of those things were completely true.

Two years ago Robin had walked into the Coffeehouse while I was singing onstage, and everything had changed. I saw my birth mother face-to-face for the first time.

And now she was lying in a hospital bed, dying.

That night I had a sociology lecture, but there was no way I could sit through it. The professor's words would have just flown through the air and dropped at my feet. Instead, I went home, dried the rain from my hair, changed into my sweats, and huddled on the living room couch in front of the TV.

The minute Bailey walked in, he knew that something was wrong. "You hate this show. Didn't you call it worse than mind candy?"

I blinked at the screen, then handed him the remote. "Change it if you want. I wasn't really watching."

He studied me. "Okay, couch potato. Want to tell me what happened with Robin?"

I buried my head in my hands, trying to collect my thoughts. "Robin is dying."

"What?" Bailey cried. "You mean—what happened?"

I looked up at him. "She's in the hospital. In a critical stage, or at least that's what the doctors say. If she doesn't get a bone marrow transplant, she'll probably live only a few more months."

He sat down next to me. "So you found all this out, and then you decided to, like, come home and sit in the dark. And you turned on this TV show that you hate just to torture yourself. Right?"

"I guess." I picked a piece of fuzz off the arm of the couch and flicked it at the TV.

"There are two ways to go with this thing. One—you can sit around feeling sorry for yourself. And believe me, there are tons of stupid things on TV to keep you company. Or, two—you can take action."

I recognized the signs. Bailey had switched into fix-it mode. That's where he gets all focused and energetic and wants to solve everyone's problems.

Well, I didn't think even Bailey could fix Robin. I grabbed a pillow and hugged it to my chest defensively. "Oh, right. Give me a minute while I run over to the lab at Berkeley and invent a cure for bone marrow disease."

"Hey, don't be mad. I'm not criticizing you or anything," he insisted. "It's just weird to see you giving up. The Sarah I know is a fighter."

A fighter? "Really?" I asked him.

Bailey nodded. "Absolutely."

Was I strong? I didn't feel that way. I wanted to fight back, but how? I was totally powerless, right? "What can I do?"

"Find a match," he answered. "Robin says you're her only family member, but maybe she's wrong. Maybe there are some distant relatives that she forgot. Maybe she's got, like, an aunt in Idaho that she never met. Or a cousin that she lost track of."

I stared into space, trying to believe that it might be possible. "Do you think . . . ?"

He nodded. "You can check it out. Use the Internet—I know you know how to do that. Do a search. Or maybe you can use a private investigator or something."

I bit my lip. It might work. Most people have relatives scattered all over the place that they aren't in touch with anymore.

"There's also the possibility of finding a donor through random testing," Bailey went on. "I mean, okay, it's a long shot. But some gambles pay off." He pointed to his chest. "I'm willing to go for a test. And I'm sure that Julia and Griffin will do it. And we can both talk to people we know at school. Post some flyers. We can start up a real campaign to get people in for testing."

Something flickered inside me as I sat there on the couch. Something bright and warm.

Hope.

"Do you really think it will help?" I asked quietly.

Bailey opened his mouth, but before he could answer I cut him off. "No, forget I ever said that. You're right. If there's one chance in a million, then it's still a chance, right?"

He nodded. "Exactly."

"Exactly." I sprang to my feet. "I can do research online from right here," I said, thinking aloud. "And I can use the library at Berkeley. And there are agencies that try to help adopted kids find their parents. Maybe they can help too?"

He spread his arms wide. "Great!"

"Great," I repeated. I headed for my bedroom, then turned back. "And, Bailey . . . thanks."

He shrugged. "Hey, if your friends can't give you a kick in the butt, who can?"

I felt so much better when I went into my room and turned on my computer. Bailey was right. I was the sort of person who needed to take action.

Where do I begin? I wondered as the monitor lit up.

Robin had told me that she grew up in Stonestown, a suburb of San Francisco. I remembered how she had talked about being in the high school drama club.

Where had she gone to school? If I could get my hands on one of her high school yearbooks, I might be able to locate a classmate who had known her, someone who could give me more details about her family. . . .

My fingers flew over the keyboard. Sometimes it takes a while to find exactly what you're looking for on the Web, but before midnight I had a list of all the high schools in Stonestown.

Sitting back on my bed with the list in my hand, I felt empowered. Bailey was right about everything. There were a gazillion things I could do.

So what if it was a shot in the dark?

There was still a chance, right?

And Robin needed every chance she could get.

Chapter 19

Here are all the yearbooks from seventy-five to eighty."

The yearbook editor at Miramar High School didn't seem to care why I was there. He plopped the cardboard carton of dusty yearbooks on a desk and wandered away.

Not like the girl at Jupiter High. I told her I was making a documentary on Stonestown, and she would *not* leave me alone. She wanted to make sure she got a starring role or something.

I flipped through the first yearbook in the stack. Nothing. I grabbed the next one. When I checked the rows of M's, I scored a direct hit.

A photo of Robin Merrill smiled up at me. My Robin. My mother.

In her senior photo her hair was lighter and shorter,

but it was definitely her. My heart started to race. Okay, I thought, trying to stay calm, so Robin went to Miramar High School. Now I have a place to start.

I quickly read her bio: *Drama Club. Pep Squad. Honor Society. Juliet to Mark Quinn's Romeo. Miramar's Flower Child.*

I wondered about Mark Quinn. Was he just the guy who played Romeo, or was he a boyfriend?

I turned to the Q's and found his picture. His handsome, smiling face didn't suggest anything. I mean, I didn't get this instant hit like: hey, it's my father!

I turned back to Robin. What did they mean by flower child? Wasn't that a sixties thing?

But something about flowers made me think back to the day Robin helped me get ready for my dinner with David. She brought those tulips over. And what did she say? Something about a flower shop . . . that her parents had owned a flower shop.

I tapped my finger on the open yearbook, wondering . . . What if the shop still existed? Of course, it would have changed hands. But maybe the new owners remembered stuff about Robin and her family.

Okay, it was another long shot. But having struck gold in the Miramar High School yearbook, I was beginning to feel lucky.

"Hey, this has been a big help," I told the yearbook editor, who was punching away at the computer. I figured he was really devoted to his work, but as I moved closer I saw that he was playing Tetris.

"No problem," he mumbled.

I spotted a stack of phone books on the bookshelves. "Are those recent?" I asked. "I need to look up a few numbers."

He shrugged. "No problem."

I pulled down the Yellow Pages for the Stonestown area and turned to F. There were a few flower shops in the area—Amy's Flowers, Flowers by Frances . . . my eyes scanned the list until I locked on to exactly what I was looking for.

Merrills' Flower Shop.

Whoa. The new owner hadn't even changed the name.

I jotted down the address, thanked the editor, then headed off to sniff around at the flower shop.

I pushed open the door and was hit by the scent— like a wall of flowers—so fresh and sweet. Roses and daisies and irises and tulips and orchids—row after row of blooms seemed to glow in the enormous refrigerator.

"Can I help you?" an older woman called from behind the counter. She had a hard, sharp chin and short gray hair.

"The flowers are beautiful," I said.

"Yes," she said impatiently. "What would you like?"

I glanced back into the case and acted on impulse. "Those pink tulips. Can you give me, like, a dozen?"

"*Like* a dozen? Or exactly a dozen?" she asked crisply.

What a grouch.

"Twelve, please," I answered. As she pulled a bucket of tulips out of the glass case, I decided to take the plunge. What did I have to lose?

"And maybe you can help me with something else," I started to ask. "I'm working on a documentary on . . . on Miramar High, and I was wondering if you know anyone who attended the school."

"What is this? Some Hollywood thing?" She began pulling tulips out of the bucket and laying them on a sheet of green paper.

"No." I smiled, trying to look earnest and innocent. "It's for a class at Berkeley."

She frowned. "My children went there, but that was years ago."

"That . . . that could be very helpful," I said quickly. "Are they in the area? I would love to set up interviews—if it wouldn't be too much trouble."

She sighed. "My son lives nearby. But my daughter . . . she moved out of town."

"Your daughter," I said, studying the woman. I stopped, staring.

No. It was impossible. I mean, Robin's parents were dead.

"Is your last name Merrill?" I asked.

"Of course," she snapped.

My heart started to beat loudly, so loud that I was sure the woman could hear it too. Was she one of Robin's relatives? There was something familiar about way she arranged the flowers, the way her hands moved.

Those hands.

So familiar. Long fingers. Slender wrists.

I glanced down at my own hands, then shoved them into my coat pockets.

"That will be fifteen dollars," the woman said, wrapping the flowers in the stiff paper.

I took a twenty-dollar bill out of my purse and

placed it on the counter, afraid that she would notice my shaking hands.

I had one more question. One important question. "For the documentary," I said, trying to keep my voice steady. "I'm compiling a roster of former Miramar students. What were your children's first names?"

She glanced at me suspiciously. "Elliot," she answered. She looked down at the flowers, taped the paper, then handed them to me. "Elliot and Robin."

Oh, God, I thought. *I'm looking at my grandmother.*

She rung up the sale and gave me my change without a hint of a smile. Then she disappeared into the back room. I walked out of the shop and stood outside, staring at the weather-beaten sign. MERRILLS'.

I should be thrilled, I thought. *I've found part of Robin's family . . . part of my family.*

Robin told me my grandparents were dead. And my grandmother was right inside that store. Alive.

Robin lied to me. Again.

I thought about all the stories Robin had told me in the past few weeks. Little pieces of her childhood. Memories of her family. Of her acting jobs. Even of my father.

Was any of it true? Had Robin said one honest thing to me since we met?

Chapter 20

I'm so blown away that you came to visit me," Robin exclaimed. Her voice sounded thick, like she was about to burst into tears. "After the way you ran out when I saw you in hematology . . . I was sure you hated me."

This was the first day Robin had felt well enough to talk to me. She looked a lot better. Her cheeks were pink, the rings were gone from under her eyes.

I didn't know what to say, how to tell her that I knew the truth, so I just thrust the bouquet of tulips at her.

"They're beautiful." She leaned back against her pillow and took a deep breath. "You remembered how much I love flowers."

"I remembered how you said that you grew up with them . . . that your parents owned a flower shop," I said, watching her reaction.

She shot me a curious look. "You remembered that?"

I nodded. "And you know what? The thing about your parents and the flower shop really helped me out. Because while you were sick, and we thought there was no way we'd find a donor, I decided to do this search. For our family."

Robin's hands squeezed tight around the edge of the sheet as the truth sank in. "Oh, my God," she said, her voice a whisper. "So you know."

"The tulips are from Merrills' Flower Shop," I said flatly.

She turned her head and stared out the window. She couldn't even look at me.

"Why didn't you tell me?" I demanded. "Why did you lie to me about your family? You told me they were dead."

Robin didn't answer. The silence stretched out between us. Was she ever going to say *anything*? Didn't I deserve some kind of explanation from her?

"In my mind they are dead," Robin finally said. She turned toward me and I could see that her face had gone completely pale.

"I haven't spoken to my parents in years," she admitted. "Twenty years. They were devastated when they found out I was pregnant. I thought they would help. I mean, in my heart I knew I was doing the right thing by having the baby, and—" She paused, as if she had run out of breath.

"What did they want you to do?" I asked. "I mean, did they pressure you to get married? Or did they want you to have an abortion?"

I couldn't believe we were talking about *me*. That baby was *me*. It just didn't seem real somehow.

Robin shook her head. "I didn't stick around long enough to really discuss it. They got the news, they freaked, and I took off. I left home and never went back."

"But now . . . now that you're sick . . ." I pointed to the monitors beside her bed. "When the doctors asked you about family members, how could you not think of them? I can't believe you didn't consider having them screened as donors."

"When you're cut off for that long, your memory becomes selective," Robin explained. "Tell a story often enough, you begin to believe it yourself. I really thought of them as dead."

She reached over to touch one of the tulips, then laughed, a harsh, ugly sound. "Serves me right. Flowers from their shop. God, life really is ironic."

I dropped into the chair next to the bed. I couldn't stop staring at her, studying her. Trying to figure out which of all the things she'd told me were the truth.

Robin met my gaze directly. "I should have been honest from the start," she told me. "I mean, about the donor thing. It's not like I was trying to trick you, but I had been away for a while, and it seemed so lame to knock on your door and just announce I was sick."

"It would have been better," I told her. "Just like it would have been better if you'd told me that I wouldn't hear from you for, like, years when you left on that road trip. I mean, what was I supposed to think?"

"I know, I know, I know," she moaned. "I'm an idiot. Just please give me the chance to make it up to you."

Robin reached out and clasped my hand. Her hand felt cold and fragile. And it was almost an exact match to mine. Same size, same shape. I could be looking at one set of hands folded together.

"I screwed up so many things in my life," Robin said, squeezing my fingers. "I know I didn't raise you, Sarah. I wasn't there for you the way a mother should be. But I can't help the way I feel now."

She pulled our linked hands to her chest, hugging them close. Her eyes were like glass, shiny with tears.

As I looked at her, I felt something catch in my throat. Suddenly, I wanted to make her feel better, but I couldn't find the words.

"I love you, Sarah," she said in a hoarse voice. "And that's the biggest surprise of my entire life. It's like this surprise gift—this incredible gift that every woman should receive before the end of her life. A daughter."

I couldn't help it. Emotion swelled inside me, brimming over. Hot tears spilled down my cheeks.

Robin pulled me close, and I buried my face in her hair. She had really turned my life inside out.

Not too long ago I had been worried about money and sex and school and my boyfriend. Now those problems seemed minuscule. Totally insignificant.

The important thing was that I had found my mother—really found her.

And I couldn't lose her again.

Chapter 21

I slowly pulled away from Robin. "There's something else we have to talk about," I told her. "I got the check."

"Did you? Oh, that's a relief," she answered. "It was one of the last things I was able to take care of before I got really sick. And it was so important to me. In a way, I think I held myself together just long enough to make sure that the money got to you."

Robin grabbed a tissue and wiped her eyes. Then she pulled out a second tissue and handed it to me.

"You know, it probably sounds weird, but I get this vicarious thrill when I think about you on that gorgeous campus," she confessed. "Since I lived in Berkeley, I know that place like the back of my hand, and it's such a fabulous opportunity for you. Keeping you in school is the best way I could possibly spend any of that money."

"Oh, Robin. That's the thing," I began. "I mean, I haven't cashed the check. Somehow, I don't know. I'm not sure that it's the right thing to do."

"Really?" She gazed up at me. "Why not?"

"It's just . . . a *huge* amount of money. And nobody gives away money for nothing. You know, there are always strings attached."

"In this case, the strings were attached years ago," Robin answered. "The day you were born. Listen, Sarah. Please, listen, because this is really important to me. I want you to keep the money. Cash the check. Let me help you with your education. It's something that a mother should do for a daughter."

It didn't sound like she expected anything from me. Maybe she was different from Mom and Dad. Maybe there were really no strings.

"You don't have to," I said.

"But I want to," she answered firmly. "Right now your education is the only thing that matters to me. Look at me, fading away in this lousy place. My life is out of control. But that money—it's one of the few things I have any control over. Promise me that you'll take it."

She sounded so sincere, and so urgent at the same time. I got the horrible feeling she was preparing to die. Sort of getting her estate in order.

"You make it sound so final," I said. I could hear my voice trembling. I hoped Robin didn't notice. I didn't want her to know how scared I felt all of a sudden.

She shrugged. "There's nothing wrong with getting your life in order. You know that stupid saying— lining your ducks up in a row. If I know you have the money to stay in school, I'll feel like I've straightened out a big part of my life."

Should I take the money? It would definitely make Robin feel good. Besides that, who was I kidding? That money would save my life—or at least my academic life.

"Okay," I said. "I mean, thank you. Berkeley is sort of my entire life right now. And thanks to you, I'll be able to stay there."

"Good." Robin smiled. "So . . . have you run into *him* on campus?"

"Him?" I shook my head, confused for a second. "Oh, you mean David? Well, yeah. I mean, we're in the same criminal justice class."

"And . . . ?" Robin prodded.

"And he sits near the window and I grab a desk by the door. David is history. It's definitely over between us."

"I'm sorry," Robin said. "I know you hoped that things would work out. And the guy *is* cute."

"Is he?" I shook my head. "You know, he acted like such a jerk that I sort of forgot about that. Yeah, David looks good. But it's only a surface-level thing."

"Mmmm. I can't tell you how many times I came across that problem with actors. A gorgeous package, but disappointing once you got a look inside."

I nodded. "And the way that he poured on the pressure. You know, the way he kept pushing for us to have sex? When I think back, I want to kick myself. I mean, the guy was so obvious. He didn't really care about me or my life or anything that mattered to me. He was in it for the physical stuff. I can't believe that I almost fell for it."

"It happens," Robin said, her eyes sympathetic.

"Believe me, it happens. But you were smarter about it than most women. The rest of us keep making the same mistake. Over and over again."

"Well, I got some good advice. Although I'm not exactly thrilled to be a perennial virgin." I held two fingers up to my forehead in the shape of a "V." "It gets a little tired, walking around with 'virgin' tattoo on my forehead."

Robin laughed. "I can imagine. But it will happen, Sarah, no question about it. And you'll be glad you waited until *you* felt ready."

I glanced over at the window. The sunlight was fading. Time for me to head home and hit the books. But I didn't want to leave.

I was afraid to go. Afraid that I would come back to an empty room and the sad faces of hospital personnel and the corny, stale excuses like: "We did everything we could for her" or "She put up a brave fight."

No . . . no way was I going to let that happen. I had fought for Robin. And I wasn't going to let her die.

"Look, I have to get going. But I wanted to leave this information with you." I reached into my knapsack and pulled out a note with an address and phone number penciled in. "I wasn't sure if you wanted to make the call yourself. Anyway, here's their phone number."

Robin shook her head, a puzzled look on her face.

I handed her the note. "It's okay if you don't feel up to it," I said. "I mean, I can call them or go see them. Whatever it takes. But I don't want to step on your toes."

She held up the slip of paper and read it aloud: "Cynthia and Grant Merrill . . . my parents?"

"You know. To call them about becoming bone marrow donors."

Robin bolted up in bed as if an alarm bell had rung. "No, Sarah. I'm *not* calling them."

"Okay," I said gently. "Then I'll take care of it. I don't mind. I mean, it could save your life."

Robin crumpled the slip of paper into a ball and tossed it onto the bedside table. "Absolutely not," she said. "I can't ask my parents for help, not after all this time. I mean it, Sarah. You've got to promise me that you won't contact them."

"But, Robin—" I protested. Couldn't she see that they were her only hope? Her only chance of survival? "Let's talk about this. The doctors say that—"

"I know what the doctors say. But this is none of their business. And it's not open for discussion. I want your word, Sarah," she insisted. "Promise me that you'll stay away from them."

I stared at her, sort of speechless, not wanting to give in. But from the way Robin sat there—her hands clenched into fists, her jaw set—I could see that she wasn't going to back down.

"Okay," I muttered. "I promise."

Chapter 22

Hey, some promises are meant to be broken," Bailey said. He ran his hand around the rim of the steering wheel.

He was right. If I kept my promise to Robin, she would die. That made my decision pretty easy.

I rolled down the window of the car and glanced across the street at Merrills' Flower Shop.

I raked my hair back from my face, trying to get everything clear in my mind. "What am I supposed to say? I mean, I already lied to Mrs. Merrill with some story about a film that I was doing. She's going to think that I'm a nut case."

"So what? Do you really care what she thinks of you?"

I frowned. "Bay, I care what everyone thinks about me."

Bailey laughed. "Yeah, you do. That's one of the

great things about you, Sarah. You want everybody to like you. You try so hard, and you don't have to. Because your friends like you even when you're not trying."

"Thanks for the analysis, Dr. Salinger."

"Anytime." He pointed at the flower shop. "So, are we going in there?"

I hesitated. "Do you think Robin will hate me?"

Bailey thought about that one. "She might be mad for a while. But you have to look at the big picture. If she's mad, she'll get over it. But her disease—there's no way she can survive that without a transplant." He turned to me and put his hands on my shoulders. "You're doing the right thing, Sarah."

"Oh, sure," I said. "Walking in on total strangers and asking for their bone marrow. Somehow it doesn't feel right."

"You're not a stranger," Bailey pointed out. "You're their granddaughter." He climbed out of the car and slammed it shut.

My mouth dropped open. Their granddaughter. Whoa.

It sounded so weird. But somehow it gave me a little rush of power. We were connected, whether they liked it or not. I wasn't some stranger asking for a favor.

Summoning my nerve, I pushed open the car door and followed Bailey across the street. He held the door open for me. "You first," he whispered.

"Chicken," I whispered back as I stepped into the shop and took in the sweet scent of flowers.

Two people were working behind the counter—an older man, who was talking on the phone, and a teenager who was covering a floral bouquet with plastic wrap. I spotted Robin's mother over by the far wall, watering some potted plants.

I walked over to her and forced myself to smile. This time I decided to stick to the truth.

"Mrs. Merrill, hi," I said. When she squinted at me, I added, "I'm Sarah Reeves. I was here the other day."

She shrugged as if to say: *So what?* "What can I get you?"

"I'm not here for flowers," I said. "I'm here to talk about your daughter . . . Robin."

Her eyes narrowed. "I have nothing to say about her."

"You need a hand, Cynthia?" the older man called.

"I'm fine," she said crisply. "The young lady was just leaving."

"Hey," Bailey said, stepping forward. "You should listen to what she has to say. It's important."

Mrs. Merrill set down her watering can and started to walk away.

"Robin . . . she's really sick," I blurted out.

"It's no business of mine." Mrs. Merrill didn't ask one question. She hurried back behind the counter and pulled a bunch of carnations out of the big refrigerator.

Bailey and I exchanged a look of desperation.

"She is *cold,*" Bailey said. "We're talking arctic freeze."

I nodded. What was I supposed to do now?

The teenager said something about a delivery, then ducked out the back door. I took a deep breath and walked over to the counter.

"You're wasting your time, young lady," Mrs. Merrill told me. She began snipping the stems of the carnations. "We have nothing to say to Robin. You shouldn't have come here."

"I had no choice," I said flatly. "I'm here because Robin needs you."

"What's wrong with her?" the older man asked me.

"Don't. Don't even talk to them, Grant," Robin's mother snapped at him.

I blinked. Of course—the older man was Grant Merrill, Robin's father. My grandfather. I turned to him, encouraged by the laugh lines around his eyes. He looked a lot friendlier than Mrs. Merrill.

"Robin needs a bone marrow transplant," I said slowly. I wanted them both to hear every word—whether they wanted to or not. "She needs a compatible donor—probably a blood relative. And because of the way things are between you, she couldn't come to you herself."

Mr. Merrill sat down in the chair behind the register. He locked his hands together. I could see his knuckles turning white.

I wished he would look up at me. If he did, I thought I'd be able to make him listen, make him understand.

"The first few years after she left, I kept hoping she would come back. Every time the phone rang, I prayed it would be her. But it's too late now," Mrs. Merrill said. She cleared her throat. "She can't suddenly reappear just because she needs our help."

"I can appreciate what you went through," I said quietly.

Mrs. Merrill stared at me, her eyes expressionless. "I doubt you have any children. And if you don't, you can't understand at all."

I grabbed the counter with both hands. I had to find a way to get through to her.

"Okay—forget it's Robin we're talking about. Pretend there's a woman in the hospital, a stranger. She's dying—but you or your husband could save her life."

Mr. Merrill's head jerked up. "That's right," I said. "Your bone marrow might be a match, Mr. Merrill."

I scribbled my name and phone number on a piece of paper and handed it to Mr. Merrill. "Please," I continued. "You could be able to save your daughter's life."

"Don't listen to her, Grant," Mrs. Merrill pleaded. "I can't do this. I just can't."

"Why did Robin send you?" Mr. Merrill asked quietly. "Are you a caseworker or something?"

"No." I shook my head. "I'm Robin's daughter. It probably sounds strange, but I'm your granddaughter. Sarah Reeves."

He flinched. "Really?"

"A few days ago she claimed she was some hot-shot producer," Mrs. Merrill told him. "She's full of lies, just as Robin was."

"That's not true." Bailey began to defend me, but I put a hand on his arm to stop him.

"This isn't about me," I said. "It's about Robin. She needs you now." I glanced back and forth between Mr. and Mrs. Merrill. "Don't you want to save your daughter's life?"

"I don't have a daughter," Mrs. Merrill cried. "My daughter died twenty years ago."

Chapter 23

Do you think I should try calling the Merrills?" I called from the living room.

"What?" Bailey called from the kitchen. "It's hard to hear over the sizzling noise these onions are making."

I scooped up my calculator, my bank statement, and a pile of canceled checks—I was in the middle of balancing my checkbook—and plopped down at the kitchen table. "I'm trying to figure out what I should do about the Merrills," I said.

"It hasn't even been a week yet," Bailey answered. "I think you need to give them a little more time to, uh, adjust to the situation."

"I guess," I mumbled. "It's just . . . I keep wondering how much time Robin *has,* you know?"

"Yeah." Bailey looked like he was trying to come up

with something else to say, something comforting. He shook his head. "It sucks."

That pretty much covered it.

I'd been visiting Robin every day. It may sound stupid, but I felt as if I had the power to will her to get healthy, to hold on, to stay alive. She looked pretty good, and she always managed to make me laugh, which is pretty amazing when you think about it.

I flipped open my checkbook and grabbed the stack of canceled checks. The top one was for my registration fees. I was all set for next semester. And I could still order takeout Chinese whenever I wanted to!

"God, I have such an easy life," I mumbled.

It wasn't just the money. Bailey and Julia had totally been there for me during this whole crisis. Yeah, they were both busy, and I didn't always see them as much as I wanted to, but when I needed them, they were *there*. And Robin . . . Robin and I kept getting closer.

"Did you say something?" Bailey asked.

"I have an easy life," I said, sort of surprised to realize it.

"Oh, right," Bailey said. "That's because you're lounging around while I'm slaving away here. Are you going to help me with the spaghetti sauce or not?"

I put my checkbook aside. "Okay, okay. What do you want me to do?"

"Chop the red pepper. And mince the garlic."

"Slave driver," I muttered.

"Hey, who requested the Salinger sauce?"

"Guilty," I admitted. "Actually, I don't mind helping. If I don't keep busy, I worry about Robin."

"Yeah." Bailey dropped a block of ground meat into the pan. "I worry about her too."

"It's crazy. I mean, my life has finally come together. And you know what? I'd give it all up in a minute. I'd give up Berkeley and anything else if it would save Robin's life."

"Bargaining," Bailey said quietly. "I used to do that after my parents died. Sometimes I'd pretend that I could bring them back if I just did something right. Like if I ace this test, or if I win this wrestling match, it'll fix everything."

I nodded. "Bargaining . . . that's exactly it. You want to strike a bargain. But all you can do is gamble. And hope." I was elbow-deep in red peppers when the doorbell rang.

"You'd better get it," Bailey said, breaking up a chunk of meat. "This is a critical stage for the sauce."

I grabbed a dishtowel and ran to the door. Through the peephole I could see two men. One looked familiar.

"Oh, my gosh . . ." I gasped as I opened the door.

Robin's father stood in the hallway, along with a younger man.

"Sarah," my grandfather said with a civil nod.

"I . . . Mr. Merrill," I stammered, feeling as if I'd been knocked off my feet. "Hello. Come in."

I stood back and let them into the living room. Bailey emerged from the kitchen looking surprised and curious. There was an awkward moment as the four of us stood there, just sort of staring at one another.

Finally, Mr. Merrill clapped a hand on the younger man's shoulder. "Sarah, this is my son," he said, adding, "your uncle Elliot."

My hands flew to my face as I saw the resemblance.

Those friendly laugh lines around the eyes . . . and those cheekbones.

"Hey," Elliot said, reaching for my hand.

Not sure what to think, I gave his hand a squeeze.

"My wife . . ." Robin's father went on haltingly. "My wife doesn't know that we're here. She's against this. She just can't forgive Robin. But we . . . we don't share her feelings."

I glanced from one man to another, afraid to believe what I thought I was hearing.

"We want to do the tests," Elliot explained. "To see if we're a match for the transplant."

My heart leapt in my chest. "Oh, my gosh. That's great!" I reached over and grabbed Bailey's arm.

I think I squeezed a little too hard, because he let out a yelp. But I didn't care.

Robin had a chance now. And I had a reason to hope, thanks to my grandfather and my uncle. Whoa. My *grandfather* and my *uncle*. Would I ever get used to that?

"Have a seat," I told them. I nearly danced to the telephone. "I'll phone Dr. Kaufman."

Chapter 24

From the moment I got Dr. Kaufman on the phone, things seemed to happen super fast. It was sort of like when you're looking out the window of a car and people and buildings and towns rush past you.

Dr. Kaufman was on call at the hospital, so he suggested that my grandfather and uncle come over immediately. I jumped in my car and led the way so that they wouldn't get lost. About six hours later, the tests were finished and we were out in the reception area.

While Mr. Merrill filled out yet another form at the nurses' station, Elliot came over and sat beside me in the waiting area.

"Let me give you my number," he said, scribbling it down on a piece of paper. "It's probably best that you don't call Dad and take the chance of getting Mom. She doesn't . . . well, just call me directly."

"No problem," I said. "Your mother—Mrs. Merrill—God, I don't know what to call her."

"Cynthia?" he suggested.

"Anyway, I never meant to upset her. I went to the shop because Robin needed help. But the minute I mentioned Robin's name, she just went—kaboom," I said, gesturing with my hands to indicate an explosion.

"Sounds like Mom. She was a lot different before Robin—" He shook his head and changed the subject. "You know, the way you talk with your hands? You remind me of her—of Robin. Her hands were always waving when she was trying to make a point. I used to tease her about it."

"Really?" I studied Elliot's face, suddenly realizing that he'd grown up with my mother. He knew what she'd been like as a kid and a girl and a teenager. "Did you guys joke around a lot?"

"Always." He grinned. "Robin had a great sense of humor. I really missed that when she left. The way we used to laugh."

"It must have been awful, having your sister disappear like that," I said.

"Yeah." He was silent for a moment, remembering. "I understood why she left. I mean, I knew that she was pregnant. And believe me, my parents are not the easiest people to deal with. But you know what made me mad? I had this ridiculous kid fantasy that Robin would come back and take me away with her. I was just fourteen at the time. Fourteen. Sort of a rebel without a cause. But you know how kids get stupid dreams in their heads."

"Yeah," I said quietly, remembering the fantasies I

had dreamed up when I'd first learned that I was adopted.

He stared off in the distance. "No matter what happens, you know, with the bone marrow, I want to see her. We were friends twenty years ago. I think we could be friends again."

"I hope so," I said.

"Do you think Dad and I could stop by her room?" Elliot asked. "I know he wants to see her too."

"Um, visiting hours are over, and they're pretty strict about it," I told him. "Maybe you should wait until next time."

Elliot nodded.

Whew! I couldn't let Mr. Merrill and Elliot just walk in on Robin. Can you imagine looking up and seeing your father and your brother standing in the doorway after twenty years or more?

Too weird.

I had to break the news to Robin. Now. I felt my stomach cramp. How angry was she going to be?

I mumbled an excuse about needing to get home, and Elliot and I both promised to keep in touch. I said good-bye to Mr. Merrill, and thanked him about a million times. Then I took the stairs down to Robin's ward.

What I said about visiting hours was true, but I had no problem slipping into her room. During my daily visits I had met most of the staff. Now that we were on a first-name basis, they were flexible about hospital rules and visiting hours.

"Hey, you," she said. She turned the sound down on the news. "What are you doing here? It's way after your bedtime," she teased.

"Bedtime? I'm a student," I said, stepping into the room. "I'm supposed to pull all-nighters. You know, study till three A.M., then sleep till noon."

Robin pursed her lips as she studied me carefully. "Don't try to fool me. I can see it in your face. Something is up."

I shoved my hands into the pockets of my sweater. "Now, don't get mad."

"Oh, God, I was right. What's going on?" she demanded.

"I know I promised not to, but I did it." I glanced down at the shiny tile floor. "I got in touch with your parents—the Merrills. And the short, quick summary of everything is that they came in to be tested—your father and your brother, Elliot."

I traced one of the tiles with the toe of my boot. Anything to keep from looking at Robin. "So . . . keep your fingers crossed. The results should be back before five tomorrow. Dr. Kaufman walked the samples down to the lab, and he put a rush order on the tests."

I forced myself to look at her. Her cheeks were flushed and her eyes flashed with anger.

Uh-oh. She was mad, really mad.

"I made a conscious choice to cut those people out of my life," she said. She twisted the sheet in her hands. "And you told me you wouldn't see them. You *promised* me, Sarah."

"I know," I admitted. "But I promised only because . . . because . . . okay, I broke a promise. So sue me."

Robin shook her head. "I can't believe you did this to me. What were you thinking?"

"I was thinking that you're way too stubborn to let go of the past and go back and ask your family for help," I answered. "So I decided to do it for you."

"I don't want their help," Robin insisted.

"See? *See?* Stubborn," I said, nodding at her. "And you know what? I'm always trying to do the right thing. To keep promises and make people happy and make people like me. But that wasn't going to work with this thing. Because you know what? If I kept my promise and did everything you wanted, you'd have no chance of finding a donor. And I would lose you. And what's the point of that?"

"The point is, this is my choice," she told me. *"My* life. I made a choice and you have to respect that."

"No, I don't," I snapped. "I won't! I won't let you go, Robin. You just became a part of my life. And you can't just walk in the door and make me care about you, and then go away!"

I flashed on the memory of Robin telling me she loved me. We were right here in this room. I could practically hear the words again.

Was it all a lie? If she loved me, how could she do this to me?

"I am not willing to give you up," I cried. "And you shouldn't be willing to give *me* up either." My voice squeaked with emotion. "You said you loved me. But if you love me, how . . . how can you give me up again?"

"Oh, Sarah." Robin stretched out her arms. I sat down on the bed and hugged her tight. I never wanted to let go.

"I do love you. I just didn't think . . . I never thought . . ." Her voice cracked. "I didn't realize what my decision would do to you."

She lifted my chin to study my face. She took a deep breath and wiped the tears off her face. "Talk about stubborn," she said quietly. "I cannot believe the way you've pushed this thing. Finding my family. Persuading them to be tested."

"I had to do something. I couldn't . . ." My voice trailed off.

"Stubborn Sarah." Robin smoothed my hair away from my face.

"Hey, it's a family trait," I said. "So . . . so will you do it?"

Robin took my hand and held it tight. "Yes. I'll do it. I'm not giving you up again. I promise."

Chapter 25

This was it—the big day.

The test results were due in this afternoon.

Unfortunately, I got stuck at Berkeley. My sociology professor completely lost track of time. She was so captivated by this case study on a street gang in L.A. that she rambled on. She didn't even get the hint when half the class started packing up their books and shuffling their feet.

Finally, one kid just got up and left and she dismissed the class. I grabbed my backpack and shot out of there like a bullet, running up the hill to the parking lot.

When I burst into Robin's room, I saw Mr. Merrill and Elliot sitting by her bed.

Can you believe it?

Somehow, I didn't think it could happen without me, but they'd gone ahead and broken the ice and gotten through all the awkward stuff. And to be honest, that was a huge relief.

I'd had enough drama in this hospital to last a lifetime.

I waved at them, trying to look casual.

"Hey, Sarah," Robin said. "Dr. Kaufman just called. He'll be here with the results in a few minutes."

"Great," I said, folding my arms and leaning against the doorjamb. It was weird how *normal* everything seemed. As if Robin hung out with her father and brother all the time.

I took a deep breath, feeling impatient. When would Dr. Kaufman get here? I checked my watch— the harlequin watch Robin bought me from the street vendor. So much had happened since that day.

I stole a look over at Robin and her father. She was showing him this photo of her covered with whipped cream and telling him about a play she was in where the villain was always throwing pies at her.

I could tell that Robin was trying extra hard to entertain her father, and it was working. He seemed relaxed and interested.

That was a good start. I mean, families don't happen overnight, right? People need to get to know each other, test each other, trust each other.

I had learned that from Robin.

And I had found a new family.

My real family. Not a perfect one. Not an adoption fantasy. But sometimes reality has its advantages. I mean, how many times do you hear fairy tales about bone marrow donors?

I couldn't help thinking about my *other* family, wondering what my relationship with Mom and Dad would be like in twenty years. Would they somehow realize they were wrong to force me to choose between them and Bailey? Or would they finally get why I was so upset that they lied to me about being adopted?

I glanced over at Robin and her dad and brother. There was obviously this . . . this *bond* between them.

And there was a bond between me and the Reeveses too. I mean, they raised me. They were there every moment of my life practically.

"Hey, how are you?" A young guy in a white lab coat stopped in the doorway, interrupting my thoughts. He didn't look much older than Bailey.

"I'm Jack Summers. Dr. Summers," he said. He shook my hand and I took in his tousled brown hair, easy smile, and warm green eyes that flickered with interest and excitement.

"Dr. Summers. Wow, that sounds weird," he admitted. "Finally, I can say I'm a doctor. I'm a resident working with Dr. Kaufman."

"Sarah Reeves," I said. "Robin is my mother." I stood back to let him into the room. "Do you need to do a test or something? We can wait outside."

"No, no, Dr. Kaufman asked me to meet him here," he said, taking a second look at me. "Wait a minute. You're the daughter who did the search, right?" I nodded. "One of the nurses told me about you," he continued. "How you did this detective work to find your mother's parents. And how you looked them up and convinced them to come in for testing."

I shrugged. "That's sort of the way it happened."

"It's an amazing story," he said. He sounded really impressed. "You are the hero of the bone marrow unit. Sheer legend. They want to hang a poster of you on the bulletin board."

"Now, that would be scary," I said, laughing.

"Not really," he said. "I wouldn't mind passing your face every day as I make rounds."

Hmmm. Dr. Jack Summers was flirting with me.

And I liked it.

"Right," I joked. "And maybe it could have those weird eyes that follow you around wherever you go."

He laughed.

There was this current of excitement between us. Sort of like an electrical field that you can't see, but if you touch it—watch out.

"So . . . Dr. Summers . . ."

"Call me Jack," he said. "I can't get used to that doctor thing."

"So, Jack," I said. "Are you specializing in this area?"

He nodded. "And when we find a donor, I'll be working with your family through the procedure and follow-up," he explained. He glanced out the door. "Hey, here's the man."

Dr. Kaufman hurried into the room and right over to Robin's bedside. "Hello, Robin," he said, taking her hand. "How's everything?"

She took a deep breath, studying his face. "You tell me."

"Good news." Dr. Kaufman smiled. "We have a match. Elliot is an excellent donor."

"Yes!" I ran over and gave Robin a hug.

A grin lit Elliot's face as he gave us the thumbs-up. "Let's do it."

Chapter 26

I don't even think you need blush. Your cheeks are this perfect pink already," I told Robin.

It was true. Ever since the surgery her skin had this healthy glow. And she had tons more energy.

"That's sweet," she said, reaching for her makeup bag. "But I am not on the sunny side of thirty anymore. I could still use a little blush."

"Hey, me too," Jack called from the doorway. "I'm way too pale."

"You do look wiped out," I told him. "What, another late-night party?"

"I wish," he muttered. "Why is it that when *I'm* on call, the entire city of San Francisco gets sick?"

Robin laughed. "Are we wearing you out?"

"I'm not complaining," he said, frowning as his beeper went off. "Did it sound like I was complaining? Not that I wouldn't love a free Saturday night—"

He looked toward me. "Another quiet dinner? A movie? An hour in couch-potato land?"

I smiled. "We'll do it again. Look, they've got to give you another day off eventually."

"Let's hope so. I've got to go find a phone." He squeezed my arm, then rushed back out of the room.

I sighed as Jack raced out of the room. We spent a lot of hours together with Robin while she recuperated from her operation.

The time we spent with Robin led to coffee in the hospital cafeteria. Then burgers at the diner across the street. Eventually we started dating.

Which is *so* great. Jack is really sweet. And he's totally low pressure. In fact, because of his hectic schedule, he's practically antipressure.

"I can't believe you're dating a doctor," Robin said. "What are you two going to do when I'm discharged? It doesn't seem like Dr. Summers ever gets to leave the hospital."

"Maybe I'll become a candy striper," I joked.

Robin shook her head. "No way. You would look lousy in a striped pinafore."

"So . . . you'd better enjoy your last few hospital meals," Elliot teased Robin that night. "After you're discharged, you're going to miss being waited on."

"Right," Robin agreed. "And I'm definitely going to miss the rubber chicken. And the fake mashed potatoes. And the vegetables. How do you think they get them so mushy?" she asked, holding up a limp green bean.

"Hours of careful boiling," Elliot said with a grin.

"I've got some crackers in my knapsack," I said.

"Sarah comes through again." Robin gave a cheer.

I smiled as I dug around in my bag. My uncle had spent a lot of time at the hospital, and it was obvious that he and Robin enjoyed each other. I felt good about that. Robin had a brother again.

I wasn't sure if she would ever be able to reconnect with her parents though.

Her dad had made a quiet effort. I mean, he had at least stopped in a few times, but I think his trips were on the sly. Because, although no one ever talked about it, we all knew that Robin's mother hadn't softened toward her. The woman was like a stone wall. Hard. Cold. Unmovable.

"Here they are." I handed Robin the crackers.

"I've got to hit the road." Elliot stood up and stole a cracker from the pack. "Oh, I'm supposed to tell you—*warn* you—about Mom. She said she's going to call you."

"Really?" Robin shifted uncomfortably. "Tell her not to bother. Tell her that—that it would threaten my health. It could set me back weeks—no, *months.*"

"No, wait—" I said. "I mean, if she's finally coming around—"

"It must mean that Dad has made her feel really guilty," Robin finished for me.

"But, Robin . . ." I said earnestly, "don't you want to give her a chance?"

"A chance for what?" Robin asked. "She's probably sharpening a silver stake to drive through my heart."

Elliot and I laughed.

"You're overreacting," Elliot said.

"Remind me again why I would want to talk to her," she insisted.

"Because she's your mother," I said.

"Oh, right," Robin shot back. "And that's important somehow?"

"Hmm. Based on personal experience, I'd say, yeah," I told her. "Your relationship with your mom is an important thing. One of those big issues in life."

"Too bad," Robin sighed. "I was kind of hoping that we could blow her off. Maybe we can send her into someone else's room. Someone who's really sick and can't talk? And she could go home to her friends and say: 'My daughter looked awful! So horrible that I didn't even recognize her.'"

"That's one way to get off the hook," Elliot said.

I studied Robin. She kept running her hands over the sheets, straightening, smoothing.

She's panicked, I realized. *That's why she won't stop joking around.*

"You really do want to talk to her. You're just scared," I said.

"Yeah," Robin admitted. "I do. I am. What can I possibly say to her? There's no way to make up for lost time."

As the room fell silent, Robin's words replayed through my mind.

There's no way we can make up for lost time.

It was true. I mean, take Robin and me. Over the past few months, a bond had formed between us. But no matter how we tried, our relationship would never be a traditional mother-daughter thing. It just wasn't the same as the bond between a girl and the mother who has raised her.

The bond I had with Mom.

Maybe someday I would call her and Dad up.

Maybe.

Elliot left, and Robin and I settled in to watch one of our favorite TV shows—this wacky melodrama about a teenage werewolf.

Yeah, I would never have a really traditional mother-daughter relationship with Robin. But I would have this. And this was pretty good.

The phone rang, and Robin knocked over her water glass. I grabbed some tissues and mopped up the spill. The phone kept ringing.

"Do I have to answer that?" Robin asked.

I nodded.

"Here goes nothing," Robin said, reaching for the phone. "Hello? This is Robin." The muscles in her face grew taut as she went on. "Yes, hi. Elliot said you'd be calling."

I stood up and went to the window as they talked. From what I could hear, they were sticking to the basics. Robin's health, the weather, the doctor's prognosis.

"Look, if you've got customers, we can talk later," Robin suggested. After a pause, she added, "Really, Mom. It's no big deal. You can . . . yes, okay. I'll hold."

I looked over at Robin. She rolled her eyes.

"She's still the same," Robin muttered to me. "Stubborn as ever."

I smiled. "Hey, we've got some stubborn women in this family."

"Speak for yourself," Robin told me, then she put the phone back to her ear. "Yes, I'm here. I mean, where else would I go? I'm here till my discharge. Well, not so much a prison. It's more like a twenty-four-hour convenience store. The lights never go out."

I slipped out of Robin's room. I figured she could

use some privacy. After all, this was a pretty important phone call. The chance to reach out to her mother.

I wandered into the waiting area and stared out the windows. A woman walked across the parking lot with a baby bundled in her arms. I looked down at them, feeling happy and sad and curious. There was something about a relationship between a mother and child. Something so complicated, yet incredibly simple.

As I watched, the woman lifted the child and gently kissed its cheek. Closing my eyes, I pressed my face against the cool glass and sighed.

Yes, sometimes it was incredibly simple.

party of five™

Join the party!

Read these new books based on the hit TV series.

#1 Bailey:
On My Own

#2 Julia:
Everything Changes

#3 Bailey:
One Step Too Far

#4 Julia
Nothing Lasts Forever